I0583402

SWEETEST OBSESSION

KRISTEN CHACE

NIMBRAVA
PUBLISHING

Copyright Page

Sweetest Obsession
© 2025 by Kristen Chace
All rights reserved.
No part of this publication may be reproduced, stored in a retrieval system, or transmitted in any form or by any means electronic, mechanical, photocopy, recording, or otherwise without the prior written permission of the author, except for brief quotations used in reviews or scholarly works.

This is a work of fiction. Names, characters, places, and incidents are the product of the author's imagination or are used fictitiously. Any resemblance to actual persons, living or dead, events, or locales is purely coincidental.

ISBN (Paperback): 979-8-9997760-0-6
ISBN (eBook): 979-8-9997760-1-3

Library of Congress Control Number
(Paperback): 2025913373

LCCN Summary:
In Sweetest Obsession, Milani "Lani" Shields is healing from a broken heart and has sworn off dating for now. Though guarded, she still believes in love and knows she'll open her heart again when the time is right. When two very different men enter her life, one promises to be everything she's ever wanted, while the other will stop at nothing to take everything from her.

First Edition
Published in the United States by Nimbrava Publishing
www.nimbravapublishing.com

Cover design by Kristen Chace
Interior formatting by Kristen Chace
Editing by ACM Entertainment
Illustrations by ACM Entertainment

Printed in the United States of America
For permissions, contact:
hello@nimbravapublishing.com

For every woman who has ever felt broken by some
warped form of love. May these pages remind you that
your softness is not weakness, your voice is still yours
and your heart may be bruised but it is not beyond
healing.
Keep the faith. Love that honors you is still possible. And
you are never, ever alone.

Prologue

I shifted uncomfortably in my seat, the silence between Michael and me growing louder by the second. The restaurant was dimly lit, intimate in a way that might have felt romantic if it weren't for the weight of everything we weren't saying. I hadn't even touched my wine. Across from me, Michael swirled his glass lazily, looking everywhere except at me.

"Michael," I began, trying to steady my voice. "I can't keep doing this. We need to talk about... us."

His eyes flicked up, dark and sharp, narrowing with irritation. "Damn, Lani. Do we have to ruin dinner with this again? You know I've been stressed."

Stressed. It was always the same excuse. Stressed because he'd lost another job. Stressed because I'd asked him to pick up a bill, or two. Stressed because I dared to expect something from him, anything at all.

I swallowed the lump forming in my throat, determined not to let him gaslight me into silence. "I'm not trying to ruin anything, Michael. But this... this isn't working."

"What isn't working?" He leaned back in his chair, crossing his arms. "I've been here, haven't I? Supporting you, cheering you on. I don't know what else you want from me."

"Supporting me?" My laugh came out sharp, humorless.

"Michael, I've been paying your rent. I've been covering your car insurance. Hell, I'm the one who paid for this dinner!"

He flinched, but only for a second. His features quickly smoothed into that infuriating calm I had grown to despise. "So now you're gonna throw that in my face? That's real classy, Lani."

My hands curled into fists beneath the table, nails digging into my palms. "You don't even see it, do you? I've been breaking my back to keep this relationship alive, and you've done nothing but take. I've put everything into us, my time, my money, my energy, and you..." My voice cracked, "you've given me nothing but excuses and lies."

"Lies?" Michael's voice rose, drawing a few glances from nearby tables. "Oh, so now I'm a liar, too? Maybe if you weren't so damn controlling, I wouldn't feel like I have to keep things from you."

"Controlling?" My voice wavered between a laugh and a sob. "Asking you to contribute is controlling? Wanting honesty is controlling? Michael, you hit me."

There it was. The words hung in the air. Heavy and undeniable.

For a moment, he didn't say anything. Then he leaned forward, his expression darkening, "You're blowing that out of proportion. It was one time, Lani. One mistake. You're really gonna throw everything away over that?"

My heart shattered all over again, the pieces scattering across the floor of the restaurant. "You don't get it," I whispered. "It's not just about you hitting me. It's about everything. You've drained me, Michael. You've taken, and taken, and taken until there's nothing left."

I pushed my chair back and stood, grabbing my purse with shaking hands. "I'm done. I can't do this anymore."

He grabbed my wrist, his fingers digging in hard enough to make me flinch.

"You're bein' dramatic," he sneered. "You really think you're gonna find somebody better than me? Please. Good luck with that, Lani. You ain't nearly as special as you think you are."

Michael nonchalantly tilted his wine glass back and forth, never breaking eye contact. "Your body? Below average at best. Took everything in me just to fake wantin' you. You think I stuck around 'cause I was into you? Nah. I needed a return on my investment.

You really believe you pulled me? With what? Your smile? Your personality? Babygirl, I saw you comin' a mile away. I knew you were desperate, and payin' like you weigh, so yeah, I hopped on for the ride. Don't get it twisted. This was always my game. You can be done, sure, but only 'cause I'm lettin' you go. Understand that."

Tears streamed down my face as I wrenched my arm free and walked away. Everything was a blur after his scalding truth. My mind was in shock, while my body moved on autopilot. One second I was standing there, feeling the last shreds of my dignity being stripped away with every word out of Michael's mouth. The next, I was outside blinking against the cold night air. My heels clattered uselessly on the pavement as I half-walked, half-ran down the street, barely able to see through the tears burning my eyes.

God, I felt like such a fool.

I wrapped my arms around myself, trying to hold something, anything together. But it was useless. I could still hear his voice, cold and clinical, replaying over and over in my head. Like I was some cash cow he was finally tired of pretending to care about. Like giving me scraps of his affection had been some kind of favor.

I gave him everything. My time. My trust. My body. And all he saw when he looked at me was someone he couldn't even stand to touch.

Humiliation twisted in my gut, thick and poisonous.

How had I let it get this far? How had I been so blind? I had wanted it to be real so badly I'd ignored every sign, every half-hearted kiss, every time he pulled away like I might contaminate him if he got too close.

I stumbled up the stairs to my building, my vision swimming. I don't even remember unlocking the door. It was muscle memory: push, turn, step inside. The second the door clicked shut behind me, my knees gave out. I collapsed onto the living room floor, not even bothering to move further. The silence of the apartment wrapped around me like a shroud, heavy and suffocating. I stayed there, curled up, my dress wrinkling under me, makeup streaking my face, my heart shattered into pieces too small to ever put back together.

The smell of the restaurant clung to me, perfume, wine, humiliation.

I buried my face in my arms, and let the sobs tear out of me, raw and broken. No careful crying, no composed sniffles, this was the ugly kind. The kind that shook my whole body until my ribs hurt. The kind that left stains on the carpet.

I felt disgusting. Used. Unwanted. Unlovable.

I hated him. I hated myself more.

I don't know how long I lay there. Minutes? Hours? Time lost meaning because the only thing I could feel was pain.

Eventually, exhaustion numbed the worst of it. But I stayed where I was, still in the dress I'd picked so carefully for him, still in the heels I'd worn as a last-ditch effort to make him see what he'd be missing. That backfired and added an additional layer of embarrassment to the ordeal. I stayed in that spot because moving meant acknowledging that all of it had been real. I didn't want to face that yet. I wasn't sure if I ever could.

That night was the end, but the scars Michael left on my life were far from healed.

In the weeks that followed, he called me relentlessly, alternating between apologies and threats. He showed up at my apartment uninvited, pounding on the door and threatening to harm me and himself. When I didn't answer, he left nasty voicemails, tearing me down for every imagined flaw.

"You're selfish, Lani. Always playing the victim. You'll never find someone like me who wants your fat ass for you."

That much, at least, was true. I'd never find someone like him again, because I'd never allow it.

But Michael wasn't content to let me go quietly. He spread rumors among our mutual friends, painting me as a manipulative, ungrateful partner who didn't appreciate all he'd done for me. I lost more than a few friendships in the fallout, people who believed his lies or simply didn't want to take sides.

It wasn't until later, when I found myself standing in the aisle of a grocery store with my card declined, that the full extent of the damage hit me. Michael had drained our shared account before I had the chance to close it. I stared at the cashier, heat rising to my cheeks as the line behind me grew restless. "I'm sorry," I mumbled, abandoning my cart and bolting for the exit.

That night, I sat in the dark of my tiny apartment, staring at the stack of bills I couldn't pay. Every sacrifice I'd made for Michael felt like a cruel joke, the universe laughing at my naivety.

But somewhere in the middle of my despair, something shifted.

This wasn't going to be my story. I wouldn't let Michael define me or my future. I had spent so long pouring myself into a man who didn't deserve me, and it was time to start pouring into myself.

Over the next two years, I rebuilt my life from the ground up. I moved to a new apartment, started therapy, and threw myself into my baking. What had once been a hobby became my salvation. It was a way to reclaim my joy and independence.

My small online shop grew steadily. Each order was a reminder that I was capable of standing on my own two feet. I swore off dating entirely, telling myself I didn't need a man to complete me. And yet, in my quietest moments, I couldn't help but wonder if there was still a part of me that wanted to believe in love. Not the kind of love Michael had offered, empty, selfish, and conditional, but something real. Something that didn't take more than it gave.

I wasn't ready to look for it. Maybe I never would be.

But if it found me...

Well, I'd cross that bridge when I came to it.

Interlude

I sat there waiting for my food, glued to my phone, scrolling until those beautiful brown eyes stopped me mid-scroll. Her smile was infectious, and those dimples melted my heart. I immediately hit follow. She was beautiful. I had never cared so much about baking in my life. To be honest, she could have been selling used tires, and I would have been interested. Her aura was amazing; even through that small phone screen, I could tell. When she looked into the camera, I felt her eyes pierce my soul. There was a connection there that I felt deep within me, pulling me to her, into her orbit. What were the odds that I had been sitting there scrolling mindlessly and found my soulmate? I had to find her live stream schedule. I could not miss another session.

"Mr. Price, your order is ready."

The cashier interrupted my thoughts, and it was a good thing too because I had been damn near salivating. In my mind, I was already seeing it all...I had to know everything about her. Her friends, what she liked, what she disliked.

I had to have her.

No... I needed to have her.

I would have her.

Chapter 1

y kitchen was my sanctuary. Or at least, it usually was. Right now, it looked like a crime scene. Flour dusted the counters like fresh snow, smudges of chocolate streaked my stainless-steel mixer, and a colorful army of measuring spoons lay scattered across the island. The air was thick with the sweet aroma of browned butter and vanilla, but my mood? Anything but sweet.

I stood there, arms crossed, glaring at the tray of brownies cooling in front of me.

"These are not cookie dough cheesecake brownies," I muttered to myself. "They're betrayal in dessert form."

I grabbed a spatula and poked at one of the squares. The dry edges crumbled slightly, mocking me. Baking was supposed to be a science, and usually, I was the scientist.

But today? Today, the experiment had flopped. My phone buzzed loudly on the counter, yanking me out of my spiral. Without even glancing, I swiped it open and answered the FaceTime call.

Lasean's face filled the screen, she glowed under that perfect lighting she always managed to find. Seriously, even in a dim room, she looked ready for a photo shoot. Her sleek ponytail was laid to perfection, and her smile was that dangerous mix of mischievous and warm. That was my girl, my bestie since beads and juice boxes. She's Lasean when she's getting on my nerves, and Sean when I remember I love her.

"Girl, are you STILL in the lab?" she asked, raising an eyebrow at the chaos behind me. "Please tell me you're coming to Othello's tonight. I will physically drag you out of that house if I have to."

I sighed dramatically and dropped the spatula. "I'm in the middle of a dessert crisis. These cookie dough cheesecake brownies are drier than a bad Black People Meet bio."

Sean cackled, so loud I half-expected my neighbors to hear. "First of all, not you roasting your own recipe! Second of all, you need a break. A cute outfit, some

cocktails, and maybe even a fine man to distract you."

I held up a hand. "Let me stop you right there. I'm deep in my *men are canceled* era. And unlike these brownies, that decision is not up for debate."

"You say that now," she teased, wagging a finger at me, "but Carlos has some handsome friends. And one of them, Myles? Girl, he's six-two, a lawyer, and he cooks. Imagine the culinary collaborations."

I narrowed my eyes. "Why do you always do this?"

"Because I love you," she said sweetly. "You deserve to be loved by someone other than your IG followers."

"My followers are supportive, drama-free, and they leave heart emojis instead of heartaches and headaches. I'm good."

But an hour later, somehow, I found myself pushing a cart through Farmers Grocery. Apparently, nothing screams girl bonding like shopping for quinoa and kale chips I wasn't planning to eat.

Sean strolled ahead, tossing bags of healthy things into my cart like she was on a mission. "I'm just saying," she said, picking right back up, "you don't have to marry the man. You can just let him take you to dinner."

"I'd rather spend my Saturday night perfecting my ganache recipe," I said, tossing a bag of chocolate chips into the cart for emphasis.

"That ganache isn't going to keep you warm at night, sis."

I stopped dead in the middle of the aisle and planted a hand on my hip. "Lasean, you're in a whole secret relationship, and I'm happy for you, I guess. But me? I'm happy where I am. No dating, no drama, just me and my business. You of all people remember the mess Michael left me in. I'm not in any rush to open myself up to more trauma, aka dating. Never mind all of that, come take a selfie with me."

Sean came over and leaned in real close and faked a kiss to my cheek. "Say ganache!"

"Girl bye!"

I took the picture and posted it. It was immediately liked by playboy285. This had been happening for the last couple of weeks. It was almost like he had an alert set for whenever I posted. No matter the time of day, he was always the first to react.

"Did your boyyyyfriend like the picture?" Sean mocked the situation.

"Shut up, he is not my boyfriend, but yes, he did."

"Yeah, well, either way, keep an eye on that. Men who are too anxious usually mean trouble...back to you being ready to start dating again."

"Sean, now you know I did not say that. I said I'm not going to date."

"You mean no dating yet," she said, giving me a pointed look.

"Fine. No dating yet." I sighed, "now can we please finish shopping before you turn into my friendly *neighbor-hood* therapist?"

By afternoon, we were finally seated at Othello's, the new dining spot that had everyone in town buzzing. The vibe was upscale, but cozy, with live jazz playing in the background. I twirled my mimosa glass between my fingers, occasionally sipping the sweet bubbly concoction, half-listening to the soft hum of conversation around us while Sean attacked her bowl of shrimp and grits like it owed her money.

"So," she said between bites, "hypothetically, if you did date again, what's the ideal man for you?"

I smirked. "Hypothetically? Someone who minds his business, doesn't ask me when I'm having kids, and can whisk without making a mess."

She laughed so hard she almost choked on her mimosa. "That's your criteria? What about looks? Personality?"

"Personality's important," I shrugged, "looks? Meh. As long as he's taller than me and knows his way around a spice rack, I'm good."

"You really are the most low-maintenance high-maintenance person I know," she said, shaking her head.

I grinned and leaned back in my chair sipping my drink. "I'll take that as a compliment."

Later, after we'd devoured our meal and dodged the topic of my love life for the fiftieth time, we ended up at the gym. I wasn't a gym rat by any means, but lately, I'd been trying to *tone up a little*. Mostly because my metabolism had started sending me subtle breakup texts. Sean was there too, for moral support, which really meant scrolling through Instagram from a nearby bench while I attempted squats.

"You know," she said, not even looking up from her phone, "squats would really make your recipes viral."

"How?" I asked, racking my weights.

"Picture it. A video of you doing squats while holding a tray of brownies. Hashtag BOOTYGAINS. You see what I did there?"

I rolled my eyes so hard I thought they might stay stuck, but I couldn't help laughing. "You're ridiculous."

"And you love me for it."

"I do. But if you post that idea, I'm blocking you."

By the time we finished and grabbed smoothies at the bar, I felt... lighter, not just from the workout.

"Alright," I said, nudging her with my cup, "maybe I'll come to Othello's next time Carlos brings his friends. But just to people-watch. No matchmaking."

Sean grinned like she'd already won. "We'll see."

Chapter 2

B y the time we got to Othello's, the dinner rush was in full swing. Jazz floated through the air, weaving in and out of the happy clatter of silverware and light conversations. The place smelled like fried chicken, waffles, spiced syrup, and strong coffee, basically heaven. For a moment, I just stood there and soaked it all in.

I tugged nervously at the hem of my green wrap dress, suddenly feeling way too aware of how it hugged my curves.

"You sure about this?" I asked Sean, lowering my voice.

She just grinned and hooked her arm through mine like I was being ridiculous. "You look amazing, so don't even start. And yes, I'm sure. Myles is exactly the kind of man who could put an end to your little 'no dating' phase. Just give him a shot."

I sighed dramatically. "Fine. But if this goes left, you're buying all my groceries for the next month."

"Deal."

The saxophones' soft hum curled around the hushed conversations drifting through the restaurant. Our booth was already set up when we walked over. Already standing to greet us was Carlos. Tall and broad-shouldered, he flashed us that kind of smooth smile that made people instantly feel at home. He pulled Sean into a hug and kissed her like she was the center of his universe. It was adorable and annoying, in that get-a-room kind of way.

Then he turned to me.

"And this must be the famous Lani," he said, his voice smooth and warm.

"Nice to meet you too. I see why Sean's been so secretive," I said, leaning closer to her with a fake smile plastered on my face. "Damn, girl."

Sean elbowed me laughing. "This is exactly why I don't tell your nosy ass anything."

Before I could fire back, Carlos gestured to the man sitting across from him. "And this is Myles."

I turned and froze.

Myles was fine. Not just good-looking, not just cute, FINE. Tall, dressed in a casual blazer and fitted jeans that looked like they were made just for him. Lean, but strong, like he could pick me up without even breaking a sweat. His dark almond-shaped eyes locked onto mine, and something in my chest fluttered. And when he smiled? Lord. I had to fight the urge to fan myself like a dramatic Southern auntie.

"Nice to meet you," he said, offering his hand.

I shook it, trying to ignore the way his warm grip sent a little jolt up my arm. "Likewise."

Dinner kicked off without a hitch. The conversation flowed with Carlos and Sean doing most of the heavy lifting. Myles was quieter, but when he did speak, his dry humor cracked me up more than once.

"So, Lani," Myles said, sipping his mimosa. "I hear you're kind of a local celebrity. Baking phenom with a big online following? That's impressive."

I shrugged, feeling a little bashful under his gaze. "Celebrity is a strong word. I just love baking. Been doing it since I was a kid. Now I get to share it with other people."

"Do you sell your stuff, or is it more for content?"

"Both. I have a shop for custom orders, but most of my energy goes into recipe development and posting behind-the-scenes stuff. That's where the magic really happens."

He smiled one of those slow, appreciative smiles that made my toes curl in my shoes. "That's cool. So you built a business and a brand from scratch. All while being beautiful, sexy, and smart... Where have you been all my life?"

I had to remind myself to breathe. This man and his charm literally just took my breath away. He said it so smoothly, but it didn't feel rehearsed. It felt... genuine. *Oh, he's a dangerous one.*

Myles and I carried on with the usual first date conversation, *even though this wasn't a date.* At least, that's what I kept telling myself. I was just people-watching, like I said.

"So are you from here, or are you a transplant?" I asked him while sipping my water.

"I'm a transplant. I came here for school and just kind of stuck around. I'm from a tiny place in North Carolina called Princeville. I'm positive you've never heard of it."

"You would be right," I chuckled. "I'm from Stonebrook, born and raised. It was just me and my mom growing up. My father passed away in a car accident before I was born, and I don't have any siblings."

Myles looked at me with the saddest, most compassionate eyes and replied,"I'm really sorry to hear that."

"It's fine. My mom tried to make sure I knew his side of the family even if he wasn't here. I had my uncles at least to step in to fill the role. How about you? What is your family situation like?"

"It's just me here. My family is all back home in Princeville with the exception of my brother and sister. My brother, the baby, is somewhere out in California being the free spirit he has always been. My sister is stationed with her husband in Japan at the moment, living their best life. I am the knee baby."

"I thought I sensed something in you. You know what they say about those middle children," I chuckled.

"No, I don't. What do they say?"

"That you are mysterious, a little rebellious, but will keep the peace if you have to. How much of that fits?" I asked with a snicker.

"All of the above. I have had a lot of practice being all three."

Sean and Carlos were in their own world. They would occasionally chime in on our conversation, but for the most part, they let us get to know each other. The conversation, combined with the eye contact, was intense.

"So if you were not an influencer, what would you see yourself doing?" Myles asked as he made himself more comfortable, leaning back in his seat.

"Probably still baking, maybe teaching culinary arts? I have always liked kids, and being in the kitchen is just such a deep-rooted part of me. I can't imagine a life where cooking or baking wasn't a routine part of my life."

"Well, that was unexpected. The kids part that is." Myles said with a slight smile.

"Don't get me wrong, I enjoy my life the way it is. I love the freedom I have, but kids are fun. I wouldn't mind being the cool auntie."

We both chuckled at that.

"How about you? Any nieces or nephews?"

"My sister is currently pregnant with her first child, so my cool uncle era is loading."

"Oh, that is exciting. Congratulations."

"What are we congratulating?" Carlos chimed in.

I almost forgot that Sean and Carlos were still here. I was so engrossed in Myles that I forgot we were not alone. I wanted to know everything about this man. If it had not been for Carlos, I would still be completely lost in him.

"Myles is about to be an uncle," I replied.

"Wow. I did not know Nova was pregnant." Carlos said, raising his eyebrows.

"Now, how did you figure it is Nova, and not Samuel?"

Carlos gave Myles the blankest stare ever. As much as I tried, I could not hold in my laughter. Obviously, there was a story there. "Okay, spill it, there has to be something behind that look."

"My baby brother might as well have been named Peter. As in Peter Pan. He lives out here like a lost boy. He is not interested in anything that could be considered adulting. I'd actually be scared if Samuel was the one having the baby."

"Yeah, I'm with Carlos on this one." I shook my head. "It sounds like Samuel doesn't need to be anybody's daddy any time soon."

Myles laughed. "So, how long have you known Sean?"

"Since the first day of kindergarten. There was this whole thing with crayons. I'm not going to get into it." I chuckled, and Sean shot me a sly grin.

"Wow, that's impressive. You don't see many friendships last long like that nowadays." Myles said. "I bet you have plenty of stories."

Now, it was Sean's turn to chime in. "I most certainly do, as a matter of fact."

Lord, what is this girl about to say? I tried to plaster the most enthusiastic grin on my face, teeth clenched, the whole nine yards. Please, Lord, if you're listening, if this prayer happens to make it past this ceiling, please, please, please do not let this girl embarrass me in front of this fine man.

"Lani, remember that time in seventh grade when Tyrell called himself liking me, and he just kept doing stupid little boy things instead of just telling me."

"Like what?" Carlos asked now interested.

"He would do little stupid stuff like pull my hair, or call me names to embarrass me. Just annoying things really. But one time in between class change he took it too far, and tripped me in front of everyone. That was the last straw. Lani was always very quiet, reserved, and proper. That day hell flew into her, because as I am getting up off the floor I see her drop her book bag, and reach all the way back to hell to knock Tyrell on his ass. Then proceeded to give him a whole speech about being a coward, and just admitting that he liked me."

The whole table laughed, even me, that wasn't so bad.

"I can't even imagine her raising her fist like that." Myles said.

"I bet Tyrell didn't bother you again." Carlos said.

"Actually they ended up dating until freshman year in high school. Those two were insufferable! His family ended up moving away which was fine with me because I got my best friend back." I playfully rolled my eyes.

As dinner went on, I caught myself sneaking extra glances at him. His laugh was rich. When I talked, he leaned forward as if he didn't want to miss a word. The attention was definitely a confidence booster. Bit by bit, I found myself being more comfortable under his gaze.

By the time the check came, I didn't want it to end.

Outside, the autumn air had a bite to it, but I barely noticed.

"This was fun," Myles said.

"It was," I agreed, smiling up at him.

He hesitated for a second, then asked, "Would it be alright if I got your number? I'd love to keep in touch."

My heart did a little happy flip. "Sure."

We exchanged numbers, and after some quick goodbyes, Sean and I made our way to the car.

"Well?" she said, practically vibrating with excitement.

"Well, what?" I teased.

"Don't play dumb. I saw the way you two were vibing."

I shrugged, trying to play it cool even though I was basically screaming internally. "He's cool. But let's see if he actually uses my number."

Turns out, he did. Later that night, a text popped up:

Myles: Had a great time today. Let's do it again soon.

Me: Same here. And absolutely.

From there, it was like the floodgates opened. We talked about everything: favorite foods, embarrassing childhood stories, career dreams. He made me laugh until my cheeks hurt. When I mentioned a recipe I was testing, he immediately offered to be my taste-tester.

Myles: Just say the word. I'll bring the milk.

Me: Bold of you to assume my desserts need milk to wash them down.

Myles: Oh, so they're THAT good? I'm going to need proof.

The banter was automatic. Effortless. It felt...different. But something nagged at me.

No matter how much we talked, Myles never asked to meet up. I dropped hints, talked about new restaurants, an upcoming food festival, but he never bit.

After two weeks of endless texting and no dates, I finally got tired of waiting around.

Sitting in my kitchen one night, scrolling through our endless thread of conversations, I decided to rip the Band-Aid off.

Me: So, when are you taking me out? Or is this all talk and no action?

I sent it before I could chicken out, my heart racing as the little typing bubble appeared...then disappeared...then appeared again. Finally:

Myles: I'd love to, but my schedule's been insane. Work's got me swamped.

I stared at the message, feeling that familiar, sinking disappointment.

Me: I get it. Life happens. Let me know when things calm down.

Myles: Definitely. You're at the top of my list.

I stared at my phone screen again, scrolling through the same old messages from Myles. Always texting. Never calling. Never actually asking to see me in person. Just flirty little exchanges, sweet nothings with nowhere to go.

I used to think maybe he was just busy. Work, life, whatever. But deep down, I knew better. If someone really wants to spend time with you, they make time. I do not do mixed signals, and texting me constantly while offering excuses why you cannot take me out is a red flag.

The longer it went on, the more uneasy I started to feel.

What was he really doing? Why hadn't we gone on a single actual date? Was he like Michael? Feeding me just enough attention to keep me interested, but never enough to feel secure?

God, that thought alone made my stomach twist.

I thought about the pictures he'd posted. The ones with his smile, so smooth. His confidence, so effortless. And then I thought about me. How I always hesitated to upload selfies unless I'd spent an hour doing my hair and makeup. How I never quite felt like I measured up to the women I imagined he usually dated.

Maybe that was it. Maybe I wasn't his type. Maybe I was just a placeholder. Something mundane. Convenient. A distraction.

What did he even see in me?

I bit my lip and stared at my reflection in the black mirror of my phone screen. My curls were frizzy from the humidity. There was a smudge of mascara beneath one eye I hadn't bothered to clean. I looked tired. Vulnerable. Soft in all the ways I used to hate.

But then I remembered.

Those two years I spent on Dr. Savant's couch taught me that my worth isn't up for negotiation. I am not defined by the attention I do or don't get from a man. I'm not a placeholder, and I'm not here to be someone's emotional plaything when they're bored or lonely. I am enough, exactly as I am. With my stretch marks, with my wide hips, my soft pudgy belly, and all the parts of me the world tried to convince me were unlovable.

I closed the message thread.

I deserved more than a man who only squeezed me in during his spare time. I deserved to be chosen. Fully, loudly, and in the daylight.

And until that happens?

I'm choosing me.

I wanted to believe him so badly. I really did. But as more days passed without plans, it was clear. Nothing was changing.

That Friday, after a hellish day in the kitchen, I FaceTimed Sean.

"He's giving me mixed signals," I said, pacing my living room. My muscles were so tight with anxiety that I felt like a snake coiled ready to strike. "One minute he's texting me like he's into me, and the next, it's like... I'm his pen pal."

"Have you called him out?"

"I did! He says he's busy. But if he's too busy to meet up, why is he texting me every day all day?"

Sean sipped her wine, her brow furrowed. "Mmm. It's giving emotional crutch. Like maybe he likes the attention, but doesn't want to actually do anything."

"Ugh. Why are men like this?"

"Not all men. Just the ones who don't know what to do with a boss chick like you," she said grinning. "What's your next move?"

I crossed my arms. "I don't know. I like talking to him. We have so much in common. He is really sweet and a great listener. But I'm not about to be some dude's ego boost. I understand taking this slowly, but I am not about to be anyone's little secret.

My mama didn't raise a placeholder. Only main character vibes over here."

"Exactly," she said. "Keep that energy."

Later that night, as I curled up in bed, my phone buzzed.

Myles: You still up?

I stared at it for a second before answering.

Me: Yeah. What's up?

His typing bubble appeared.

Myles: There's something I've been meaning to tell you...

My stomach twisted.

Me: Okay... I'm listening.

The typing bubble popped up.

Then disappeared.

Then... nothing.

I waited.

Five minutes.

Ten.

An hour.

Still nothing.

Frustrated and exhausted, I tossed my phone onto the nightstand and turned off the light.

Whatever he had to say... he could say it tomorrow.

If he ever got around to it.

Chapter 3

I stared at my phone, frozen in disbelief. Myles' text sat on the screen, mocking me:

Myles: There's something I've been meaning to tell you... I'm married.

Married.

Not separated. Not "we're living in different states, and trying to figure things out."

Full-on married.

The kind of married that came with wedding bands, joint bank accounts, and a Costco membership. The kind that came with PTA meetings, soccer games, and a family subscription to the latest kid friendly streaming service.

I blinked. Twice. Then a third time.

"THIS MOTHER, " I cut myself off, sucking in a sharp breath. My fingers flew across the keyboard, fury giving them wings.

Me: Married? Like, married married? With a wife? A house? Kids?

His response came fast, like he actually thought he could smooth this over.

Myles: Yeah... I was going to tell you.

"Tell me when?" I muttered, pacing the living room like a caged tiger. "After I baked you anniversary cupcakes?"
I stabbed at my phone, typing furiously.

Me: So you've been texting me for weeks now. Flirting. Leading me on. While you've got a whole family at home?

The reply came instantly, like he thought he had a fighting chance to save whatever this was we had going on.

Myles: It's not like that. My wife, and I... we're not in a good place. The marriage is not salvageable, but I admit I have not done my part in communicating it's finality.

I snorted so hard I almost choked.

Me: OUTSTANDING, you're taking accountability. Tell me something, does your WIFE know your marriage is not salvageable? Did you even stop to think about me, and how this would affect me?

Silence.
Good. I hoped it stung.
Then, a buzz.

Myles: I'm sorry. I never meant to hurt you.

A dry, humorless laugh tore from my throat. I set my phone down before I threw it against the wall.

By the time Lasean showed up the next morning, I was in full-blown rant mode, pacing the kitchen with a cup of coffee clutched in one hand, my other, gesturing like I was orchestrating a symphony of rage.

"I'm telling you, Lasean," I snapped, "this man is married. Like, MARRIED married."

Lasean sat at the kitchen island, her mouth hanging open. "Wait, wait, wait. He told you he was married?"

"Yup."

"And you had no clue?"

"None," I said, throwing my free hand in the air. "He hid it better than the Holy Grail in the Da Vinci Code."

Lasean tried not to laugh. "Damn. That's... I don't even know what to say."

"You can start by not laughing!"

"I'm not laughing at you, or the situation, but you know I love a good movie reference. Sorry."

"Well, forget all of that! Why didn't YOU say something? You're the one who set this whole thing up!"

She raised her hands in defense, "Hold up. You're blaming me now?"

"Who else am I supposed to blame?" I snapped. "You dragged me out of my peaceful life and shoved me into dinner heaven only for him to turn out to be a lying dog!"

"I didn't know he was married, Milani! I've never seen him with a woman. Never heard Carlos mention one."

"Didn't know," I scoffed. "But did you even bother to check?"

Her face fell. Guilt flashed across her features.

"Look," she said quietly, "I didn't do a background check or anything, but Carlos vouched for him. Carlos has never given me a reason not to trust him. I would think that if he knew he was married, he would tell me when I suggested it."

"Well, congratulations to Carlos for being absent-minded as hell," I muttered, rolling my eyes. "Now I'm stuck picking up the pieces of my dignity because your boyfriend's bestie turned out to be a walking red flag."

Tension clung to the room, simmering just under the surface. I hated feeling this way with Laean, but the betrayal, direct or not, still burned.

After she left, I spiraled. Anger, sadness, disbelief, all tangled up inside me. I turned to my most reliable coping mechanism: baking.

Flour flew as I whipped up a batch of triple chocolate brownies, pouring every ounce of frustration into the batter. But not even the smell of melting chocolate could erase the hollow ache in my chest. My apartment was usually my sanctuary, but right now it made me feel stifled... alone. The silence reminded me that it was just me and my appliances; my only connection was the whirring of my mixer or my clanging of measuring spoons.

By the time the brownies were done, I'd eaten two spoonfuls of raw batter and drained down half a bottle of rosé. My phone buzzed on the counter I didn't bother checking...of course it was playboy285 liking my latest post. It was like clockwork. The sugar and alcohol buzz left me feeling reckless, which is exactly how I ended up staring at an online dating profile screen about to risk it all for something tall, dark, and handsome, like that ever worked in my favor.

The cursor blinked at me, daring me to do something.

It had been two weeks since Myles's confession. Two weeks since everything I thought could be, wasn't. The sting of it still sat heavy on my chest, a stubborn weight.

I had cried. I had cursed. I had called Sean more times than I could count, replaying every moment with Myles, hunting for signs I missed.

It was Michael all over again.

The detachment.

The secrets.

The betrayal.

But something was different this time.

Myles may have been a dog, but if I was honest with myself, he didn't have the same cruelty Michael did.

I had survived Michael.

I had clawed my way out of that mess, out of the manipulation, the gaslighting, the emotional and financial drain. I remembered standing in front of the mirror, months after it ended, staring at a stranger.

Thinner. Tired. Hollowed out.

But I was still standing, despite it all. I rebuilt my life from the ground up, starting with my self-esteem. With my newfound confidence, I grew my business. I created a sanctuary in my kitchen that could keep me grounded when my resolve started to slip. I chose myself, again, and again, even when it was hard.

I hadn't given up on love.

Because giving up would mean Michael still had power. It would mean his lies, his abuse, his destruction had won. And I refused to let that be my story.

I wanted love. Real love. Not the kind you had to shrink yourself for. Not the kind built on secrets.

I wanted partnership.

Honesty.

Laughter in the kitchen.

A hand to hold when the nights got long.

I hovered my thumb over the submit button, feeling a bittersweet smile tug at my lips.

"I'm still here," I whispered to the empty room. "And I still believe."

Click.

Profile submitted.

Single baker. Lover of sarcasm and carbs. Looking for someone who knows the difference between a macaron and a macaroon.

The first guy was shirtless, holding a fish the size of a toddler. Hard pass.

The second guy called himself a "crypto king" who could "teach me how to escape the matrix." Swipe left.

The third guy was decent-looking. An accountant. He liked dogs and hiking. I hesitated, then swiped right.

A match.

Before I could even overthink it, a message popped up.

Greg: Hey, Lani! Your profile caught my eye. What's your favorite thing to bake?

Oh, great. An icebreaker.

Me: Depends on my mood. Right now, brownies.

Greg: Solid choice. Do you eat them with ice cream, or just plain?

I smirked.

Me: Both. I'm an overachiever.

The conversation stayed light… until he mentioned his favorite brownie recipe involved sprinkles.

Me: Sprinkles? In brownies?

That's a red flag.

Greg: I like the color.

I swiped left mid-conversation. "What is he, four? I have no time for toddlers."

The next hour was a blur of swiping, laughing, and occasionally yelling at my phone. I matched with a few more people, but no one really sparked anything in me.

Until I saw him.

I stopped mid-scroll.

Gorgeous.

Chiseled jawline.

Deep brown eyes.

A smile that could light up a room.

His bio was short, but it hit me right in the heart: *Just a guy looking for someone to share late-night pancakes with.*

I swiped right.

It's a match.

My heart skipped a beat when he messaged almost immediately.

Darius: Late-night pancakes, or waffles?

Me: Pancakes, obviously. Waffles are just pancakes with a superiority complex.

He sent back a laughing emoji, and just like that, the conversation flowed, fluid, funny, and natural. For the first time in weeks, I felt something close to excited. By the end of the night, I was smiling, so hard my cheeks hurt. But as I lay in bed, staring at the ceiling, the excitement started to fade. Myles's betrayal still loomed in the back of my mind like a shadow.

What if Darius was too good to be true, too?

Can I really put myself through getting to know someone else, only to be disappointed in the end?

My phone buzzed.

Darius: You free for pancakes tomorrow night?

My heart raced.

Was I ready for this?

I typed out a response, paused, and deleted it.

My finger hovered over the keyboard, torn between excitement, and fear.

Chapter 4

Carla's Diner was bustling as usual, its neon sign casting a pink and blue glow across the sidewalk. I stood outside, clutching my bag like a lifeline while checking my reflection in the window. I'd picked a black midi dress that hugged my curves just right, paired with ankle boots to give me a little extra height.

"Girl, pull it together," I muttered under my breath, smoothing my hand over my hips.

Just as I reached for the door, a voice called out behind me, deep, velvety, and impossible to ignore.

"Milani?"

I turned and immediately had to tilt my head up. Damn. He was tall. Darius stood at least 6'4", and he looked even better in person than he did online. His mahogany skin glowed beneath the city lights, and that smile, perfect except for a small, charming gap between his front teeth, knocked the breath right out of me.

"Wow," he said, giving me a once-over with that disarming grin. "You're stunning."

I felt my face heat up as a blush crept up my neck. "And you're tall," I shot back, trying to sound playful instead of flustered.

He laughed, stepping closer. "I promise, I'm not as intimidating as I look."

"We'll see about that," I teased, leading the way into the diner.

Carla's smelled like heaven, maple syrup, sizzling bacon, and fresh coffee all mingling in the air. We got a cozy booth near the window, and before I could even glance at the menu, Darius ordered us both a stack of their award-winning buttermilk pancakes.

"You weren't kidding," he said, glancing around. "This place is packed."

"I told you," I said, sliding my menu aside. "Carla's pancakes are legendary. You've seriously been missing out."

"Well, I'm here now. Thanks to you."

There it was again, that smile. It was doing dangerous things to my insides, so I focused on the table, hoping to steady myself.

"So," I said, nudging the conversation into safer territory, "tell me about your sports memorabilia shop."

His whole face lit up. "It's my baby. Been open for six years now. We specialize in rare collectibles, signed jerseys, championship rings, vintage game footage on tape. Pretty much anything a sports fan could dream of."

"That actually sounds amazing," I said, genuinely impressed. "What got you into that?"

"My dad," he said, voice softening. "He was obsessed with sports. We used to collect cards together when I was a kid. The shop was his, actually. I grew up there. He passed away a few years ago, but keeping the shop going is my way of keeping him alive. It's all I have left of him. It's the most important thing in the world to me."

My chest tightened. "That's beautiful, Darius."

He met my eyes. "Thanks. What about you? You bake, right? What got you into that?"

I grinned. "That's my mom's fault. She couldn't bake to save her life, but she let me take over the kitchen when I was little. By the time I was twelve, I was making cakes for every family gathering. When social media came along, I just... ran with it."

"And now you're an influencer."

"Apparently," I said with a laugh. "It's still weird. Strangers message me for advice like I know what I'm doing. Half the time, I'm just winging it."

"You're humble," he said, eyes locked on mine. "That's rare."

"I don't consider it humble, I'm just more surprised by it than anything. I love baking, and I love people. I am blessed to take two of my loves, and be able to make a living."

"Good deal, so what do you think your next move will be?"

"My dream is to open my own bakery. A real lush trendy space that can serve as both a bakery and café. I'm big on vibes, and as much as the food is important, I believe the ambiance must fit as well. How about you?"

"I'm a simple man like my father, as long as I can make enough for my family to be comfortable and happy, that is enough for me."

"So where are you from? Born and raised in Stonebrook?"

"Yes, all my life." He replied while sipping his drink.

"Me too. Which high school did you graduate from? What year? We are close in age, so we might have run into each other at some point. You might even show up in one of my yearbooks. It is a small world after all."

"I was actually homeschooled, so unfortunately you won't be able to track down any of those awkward teen photos of me." He said with a sly smile.

His voice was so warm, I felt my stomach flutter again. I was grateful when the pancakes arrived, stacked high, with all their glorious fluffiness, giving me a reason to look away.

The next hour flew by in a blur of laughter and polite conversation. I found myself opening up to Darius in a way that felt so natural, so effortless. We bonded over our love of old-school R&B, cheesy action movies, and a shared hatred for walnuts in brownies.

"Wait," I said, nearly choking on a laugh. "You've never seen Coming to America? How is that even possible?"

"I don't know!" He said, throwing his hands up. "I guess I missed the memo."

I held out my hand, "Give me your card."

He looked at me completely puzzled.

"Your black card, now. Coming to America is like a staple for every Black household in the 90s. Eddie was in his prime at that time. I'm pretty sure my mom made me watch all of his movies, whether they were age-appropriate or not." I chuckled to myself, thinking about those movie nights with my mother.

"Well, my parents were a little on the strict side, so a lot of the culture I didn't get to experience as a kid." He replied, a little more sullen than the conversation required.

Touchy subject, noted.

"Oh, we're fixing that," I declared. "Movie night. My place. Non-negotiable."

He raised an eyebrow, smiling. "Are you inviting me over already?"

I hesitated. "Well, I..."

"I'm kidding," he said, reaching across the table to gently touch my hand. "I'd love that."

My heart skipped at the contact, but I played it cool.

After he paid, he insisted on walking me to my car. The night air felt crisp and refreshing after the warmth of the diner.

"You know," he said as we reached my car, "this was the best first date I've had in a long time."

I arched a brow. "Oh? And how many first dates are we comparing this to?"

He laughed. "Not as many as you're thinking. I'm picky."

"Good to know," I said softly. "This was nice. Really nice. What do you have planned after this?"

"Nothing really, maybe go into the shop to work on some inventory. Nothing that can't wait until tomorrow. Why what's up?"

"I was just thinking about that movie night. You want to come back to my place and see what you missed?"

Darius stepped closer, his expression turning serious. "Lani..."

The way he said my name sent a shiver down my spine.

"Yes?"

"I'd really like that."

I felt my breath catch. "You're not just saying that, are you?"

He chuckled, shaking his head. "No. I genuinely want to spend time with you, to get to know you. Not to mention I have to see what the hype of this movie is about."

"Good," I said, unlocking my car. "Because I'd like that too."

Butterflies and nerves filled the drive home. When I pulled into my complex, I whispered to myself, "it's now or never."

"Come on in," I said with unexpected confidence, surprising even myself.

He looked at me for a moment, then nodded. "You definitely don't have to ask me twice." The sly grin he gave had me feeling things in places I forgot even existed.

Inside, I kicked off my boots and led him to the living room.

"Make yourself comfortable," I said, heading for the kitchen. "I'll grab us some wine."

When I came back, he was admiring the shelves of cookbooks and framed family photos lining the walls.

"You've got a beautiful home," he said, accepting the glass I handed him.

"Thank you. It's my little sanctuary."

We sat on the couch, and the conversation resumed like it hadn't missed a beat. As the night wore on, the space between us kept shrinking, bit by bit.

Then, Darius reached out, brushing a stray curl from my face.

"You're something else," he murmured.

My heart pounded. His hand lingered near my cheek, and the air between us buzzed with electricity. Our faces were inches apart.

"Darius..." I whispered, my voice trembling.

"Tell me to stop," he said, eyes locked on mine.

I didn't.

When our lips met, the kiss was soft at first, then deepened quickly. It felt like years of longing exploded into that single moment. His hands found my waist, and pulled me closer. I melted into him.

For a moment, I let myself get lost in it, the warmth of his touch, the way he murmured my name against my lips. But then, reality crashed in like a cold wave.

"Wait," I said, pulling back, breathless.

He looked at me, concern flickering across his face. "What's wrong?"

"I... I can't do this," I said, standing, and hugging myself. "Not like this. Not yet."

He stood too, giving me space. "Lani, it's okay. I didn't mean to..."

"It's not you," I said quickly. "It's me. I'm just not ready."

He nodded, slowly and steadily standing. "I understand."

"Do you?" I asked, searching his face.

"Yes," he said, firmly and sincerely. He turned and made his way to the front door. "I'm not going anywhere. When you're ready, I'll be here. I'm going to be honest with you though after that..." He ran his hand down his face. "I can't be here right now in this moment. Right now I need to find a cold shower." He chuckled.

His words made me giggle at first. Then I took in the underlying sincerity and my throat tightened. I watched from the doorway as he left, disappearing into the night.

I closed the door behind Darius, and leaned against it, letting out a long breath like I'd been holding it in since dessert. The air in the room suddenly felt different, too still, and quiet.

Girl, what was that?

He hadn't even had enough time to make it to his car yet, and I was already in my feelings. Not because it was a bad date. It was a good one, almost perfect. Everything, including his scent, had me on go. Oud, spice with a hint of smoky vanilla. I don't know who made the cologne, but it should have come with a warning. My knees want to give out just reminiscing about it. Even though he smelled and looked absolutely delicious, it was no excuse for my behavior. I almost went through with it.

I almost gave up my cookies.

On the first date.

I dropped my head back against the door with a dramatic sigh. "Lani, what were you thinking?" I whispered to myself.

I know it's been a while, two years at least, maybe longer, but damn, that doesn't mean I need to be out here acting like I'm in heat just because a man made eye contact, and let me ramble. Was I really about to let all this self-worth I've been working on unravel over one good-smelling, sexy man, and a stack of pancakes?

Do I look desperate now?

I hate that I even care, but I do. I've spent so much time trying to protect my peace, build something solid for myself, and here I am spiraling because a man looked my way. Granted, he did look at me like I was edible.

Maybe it wasn't just that I felt easy. Maybe I believed I wasn't enough, and my body was the sick trade I had to make for even the smallest bit of attention.

I walked into the bathroom and caught my reflection. Still dressed up. My light makeup was still fresh from the date. I put it on like armor. Now sitting here with just me and my thoughts, all I could see were flaws. My thighs. My arms. The roundness of my stomach pressing gently against the fabric. My stretch marks felt more pronounced than usual. That stupid voice in my head, the one that sounds just like Michael, started whispering. He probably likes women with flat stomachs. Toned arms. S m a l l e r everything.

It's like no matter how confident I think I am, moments like this strip my confidence bare until nothing is left but my insecurities.

I caught myself.

I gripped the edge of the sink and looked myself in the eye.

I decided my value.

I am THAT GIRL.

I am desirable.

No man can change the way I feel about me.

Especially not Michael. I'm worthy of love, love from myself and my man. I'm not about to sleep with someone just to keep their interest.

If he's really worth it, he'll wait. Not just for my body but for my comfort. My readiness. My yes, when, and if I give it.

If he doesn't?

That tells me everything I need to know.

I slipped out of my dress and wrapped myself in my favorite robe. Just as I was about to climb into bed, my phone buzzed. I glanced at the screen, and my stomach dropped.

Myles: "Hey, Lani. It's Myles. Can we talk?"

Chapter 5

She was my everything. My good girl. The moment she walked up to Carla's, *damn*. That black dress, the way it clung to her like it had been made for her body. Soft and powerful all at once. She didn't just walk in; she commanded the room without even trying. Every man looked, but she didn't look back. Not once. She was focused. Present. Polished. Like a woman who knew exactly who she was. And the moment her eyes met mine, I knew, that's her. That's my person.

Milani.

Even her name sounded expensive. Like silk and diamonds.

I watched the way her lips curved when she laughed at something I said. She laughed easy, but not too easy. There was a hint of something behind it, though. Hurt maybe. She didn't talk about it, not directly, but I could see it. She was guarded. The way she tilted her head, always slightly away when she spoke about anything personal. She was still healing. And that was fine. I could be patient.

I'm good at waiting for what I want.

And her? I want her. No, I need her.

She thinks this was just a date. A little dip back into the dating pool. Something casual. But she'll see. I'm different. I listened. I paid attention. The way she likes her tea, light sugar with a lemon wedge. The way she looks away when she's thinking too hard. The way she absentmindedly runs her finger along the rim of her glass when she's nervous.

Most men don't catch that kind of thing.

But I'm not most men.

Most men don't deserve her. The one who hurt her doesn't deserve to breathe.

I deserve her, and I will do anything to prove it.

Anything.

I'll give her what she needs. My body, my soul, my love, hell even my freedom if she requires it. She won't have to wonder with me. I'll show her she can rely on me, trust me, lean on me. She'll come to see I'm the safe place she's been looking for. The one she didn't even know she needed.

She'll be mine.

Not in a possessive way, not like that. Just... meant to be. Destined, really. It's just a matter of time.

The first date went exactly how it was supposed to. I slipped a little something in her bag so I could make sure she's safe. I showed her the best version of myself. Not fake, more like curated. I could tell. This connection? It's real. It was there from the start. This date was a success. I checked off all the boxes.

She's going to try to resist it, probably. That's okay. I'll make it easy for her to fall.

She won't even realize she's doing it.

Not until she's already mine.

Chapter 6

The bright light and soft random Top 100 pop song coming through the speakers were surprisingly soothing. Sean and I alternated talking and singing along, pushing our carts like little old ladies. As we hit the body care aisle, we sniffed, compared, and looked at ingredients, filling our carts up with body butters, body washes, and every kind of scrub imaginable. They made great cart mates with the wine we didn't need but always bought anyway. Our heels clicked in rhythm over the glossy tile, the sound a familiar beat to our girls' night tradition.

"I'm telling you," Sean said, holding up a glittery face mask. "This right here is either going to make me look twenty-one again or give me a rash."

I laughed and side-eyed her hard. "I'm gonna go with rash for one hundred, Alex. Please put that back."

She put it back on the shelf dramatically. "See? That's why I love you. Always my voice of reason. You're like that little roach that sat on what was his name's shoulder?"

"Please do not tell me you're talking about Pinocchio."

"Yeah, that's it!"

"Sean, he was a damn cricket! His name was Jiminy Cricket!"

"I do not do bugs. If it's little, crawling, flying, or anything in between, baby, that is a roach." Sean did this dramatic-ass shiver and brushed at her arms as if just talking about the damn things made her feel them crawling on her.

I just chuckled and rolled my eyes, because she was impossible.

As we made our way through the store, browsing, wrapping up our trip, we turned the corner near the refrigerated drinks, heading toward checkout. I froze, just for a second. Standing at the end of the aisle, a bottle of water in one hand and what looked like beef jerky in the other, was Darius.

My smile faltered. It was automatic, muscle memory, but my brain was scrambling. What was he doing here? Darius didn't live on this side of town. Why would he come all this way through traffic to buy water and beef jerky?

He smiled when he saw me, that slow, smooth grin that made my stomach flip.

"Lani," he said, stepping closer. "Wow. Fancy seeing you here."

"Yeah," I managed, plastering on my best polite smile even as every instinct in me prickled. "Small world. What brings you over here on this side of town?"

"I had to meet with a collector this afternoon. He was trying to unload some vintage baseball cards. They turned out to be fake, so I thought the drive was wasted until I saw you."

I blushed.

Sean, sensing my shift in energy, stepped slightly closer. She eyed Darius the way she always assessed danger, head to toe, slow and deliberate.

"Oh, where are my manners? This is Sean," I said quickly. "My best friend. Sean, this is my...friend Darius."

I thought I saw his eyes flash, but it had to be the lighting.

The pause before "friend" tasted sour in my mouth. He wasn't my boyfriend. We have only been on one date. Yes, I tried to climb him like a tree that night, but still, it was only one date. Why was I even fighting with myself on what to call this man?

Sean nodded slowly, while warily offering her hand. "Hey."

That's my girl. I love her life, but I must admit she is very protective of me. I could tell she wanted to follow my lead, but

Sean has serious trust issues when it comes to me and my judgement in men.

Darius took her hand and looked her over like he was sizing her up, then turned his eyes back to me. "Didn't know you came here," he said casually. "I pegged you for a Costco girl."

"I don't usually." I loosened my grip on the shopping cart. I didn't know I was about to break in half. "Just here for a girls' night. Kind of our thing."

"Is that right?" He nodded, then lingered a beat too long.

I watched his eyes roam from my curls down to the curve of my waist like he was collecting a memory. If I didn't know any better, I would think he wanted to take me right here in this store. Heat rose to my cheeks at the thought.

Sean cleared her throat loud enough to break glass. Breaking me out of my shameful thoughts.

"Well," I said, shifting my weight to my other foot, "we've got a full cart and a long line ahead, so…"

"Of course," Darius said. "It was really good seeing you. I'm going to text you later to see if we can put something on the books."

"Yeah. You too, that would be great." I turned, pulling Sean with me toward checkout. I didn't look back, but I felt his eyes on me the entire way. I must admit, I threw a little Loretta Divine in my step for good measure.

Only when we were out of earshot did Sean mutter, "You didn't tell me he was that fine."

"You didn't ask."

"Be careful with that one though, the pretty ones can be tricky."

I sighed. "Hell, the facially challenged ones can be too, I just have to watch out for them all."

Chapter 7

I sat on my couch, phone in hand, staring at Myles's message like it might disappear if I blinked too hard. I'd already read it three times, and each time left me feeling more conflicted than the last.

> *Myles: I know I have no right to ask for your time, but I owe you an explanation. Please, Lani. I'm sorry.*

I exhaled, tilting my head back against the cushions. My first instinct had been to block him, delete, ignore, move on. He'd lied. He'd led me on. He was married. But something in his words, maybe the vulnerability, or maybe that annoying part of me that always roots for the underdog, made me hesitate.

Before I could talk myself out of it, my fingers moved on their own.

> *Me: I'm listening. Make it quick.*

His reply came faster than I expected.

Myles: Thank you. My marriage is... complicated, to put it mildly. My wife has been having an affair for over a year. I didn't know until recently. I guess I've been in denial about how bad things really were. Meeting you was the first time in a long time I felt like I could be happy again, honestly. That doesn't make what I did right, but I wanted you to know the truth.

I hovered over the keyboard, not sure what to say. Half of me wanted to tear into him for being selfish and dragging me into his drama, but the other half, the empathetic half I wish would mind its business, felt sorry for him.

Me: So, what now? You try to date while you're still married? How exactly does that work? I can tell you now, that doesn't sound like it's going to work, especially not with me.

Myles: No, of course not. I just... I don't know. I'm trying to figure things out. I know I was selfish, but when Carlos asked me to go, I really did not see the harm in just having a meal together. I admit, though, that my situation should have been made clear to you in the beginning, and for that, I sincerely apologize. I really enjoyed the connection we had. Even if we can't be anything else, I'd like to at least be your friend.

Friend? I raised an eyebrow and almost laughed out loud. Seriously?

But there was something about the way he said it, the honesty, the desperation, that gave me pause. He sounded like a man grasping for something, anything, just to stay afloat.

With a heavy sigh, I typed back:

Me: Fine. But just friends. That's it.

The next day, he invited me to lunch. To apologize in person. I hesitated, I stalled for hours, but curiosity eventually won. I told myself that meeting in public was harmless and that hearing him out didn't mean anything.

We met at Reel Catch, the seafood place that's always packed on weekends. The second I walked in, the smell of fried fish and garlic butter hit me square in the face, and my stomach growled. Myles was already seated in a booth near the back, looking nervous but, ugh, still undeniably handsome in a navy button-down and dark jeans.

"Hey," he said, standing as I approached.

"Hey," I replied, sliding into the seat across from him. I kept my tone cool. Neutral. No use making this easy.

"Thanks for coming," he said softly.

"Let's just get this over with," I muttered, flipping open the menu. "I'm starving."

It started out awkward. He tried apologizing again, but I cut him off.

"Look, you already said sorry. Let's just eat and keep it light."

He nodded, visibly relieved. We placed our orders: shrimp and grits for me, the Catcher's Feast for him. We slowly slipped into a rhythm that didn't feel quite as tense.

When the food came, I nearly choked at the sight of his plate. It looked like a deep-fried seafood mountain: shrimp, scallops, clams, oysters, catfish. The works.

"Wow," I said, shaking my head. "You're really going for it, huh?"

"I didn't eat breakfast," he said, picking up a shrimp.

"Sure," I smirked. "If you say so."

And then it happened. He reached for the ketchup, cocktail sauce, and tartar sauce, then proceeded to drown his entire plate in some kind of chaotic, unholy mixture.

"Oh no." I held up a hand. "What are you doing? You're ruining it!"

"What?" he asked, looking genuinely confused.

"Ketchup, cocktail sauce, and tartar? All together? On all that? You're eating like a three-year-old."

He laughed, completely unbothered. "Don't knock it till you try it."

"It's giving Norman Bates. I'd rather not," I said, wrinkling my nose. "That's disrespectful to seafood everywhere. The only acceptable condiments are hot sauce, tartar, or cocktail. Not all three at once."

Our banter continued through the rest of the meal. I hated how simple it was. Myles took my teasing in stride, and by the time we finished eating, the awkward tension had faded. It almost felt...normal.

When we stepped outside, standing by the curb to say goodbye, I felt a weird little tug in my chest, like something unresolved was still hanging in the air.

"Thanks for hearing me out," he said quietly.

"Don't thank me yet," I replied, folding my arms. "We'll see if you're worth keeping around as a friend."

He chuckled. "Fair enough."

I walked to my car, still unsure if I'd made the right decision. Just as I opened the door, my phone buzzed.

Darius: How's your day going, beautiful?

My heart fluttered and then sank. The timing was... awful. I'd just spent the afternoon with one man... and now another was texting me?

"Great," I muttered to myself. "Now I'm officially in the middle of a mess."

Myles and I were just friends, or at least trying to be, but I'd be lying if I said there weren't any lingering feelings. Maybe *"feelings"* was too strong: more like nagging thoughts of what we could have been. Still, it left me feeling less than stellar to be mourning a *could-have-been* while snuggled up to another man.

I slid into the driver's seat, and stared at my phone for a second before replying.

Me: Hey! It's been good. How about you?

I hit send, and tossed the phone onto the passenger seat with a sigh.

The whole drive home, my mind pin-balled between Myles's story, and Darius's text. I hadn't felt this off-kilter in a long time.

When I got home, I threw a blanket over my lap, and tried to settle, but my phone buzzed again.

Darius: Good! I was hoping we could hang out again soon. What's your schedule like?

I bit my lip. My knee-jerk reaction was to say yes, to dive into something fresh and uncomplicated. But was it really that simple?

The mess Myles stirred up hadn't fully settled. I hated that it still made me feel things I didn't want to feel. I typed and deleted a few different responses before finally sending:

Me: Let me get back to you. Things are a little crazy right now.

And the moment it sent, I regretted it.

I leaned back on the couch and stared at the ceiling. "What the hell am I doing?"

My phone buzzed again, but I ignored it this time. I needed space to think, to breathe, to figure out what I actually wanted.

Later that night, just as I was drifting off, another message came through.

Myles: Hey, I just wanted to say I really appreciated today. It meant more to me than you know.

I stared at the screen, my heart twisting. The feelings I thought I'd buried weren't buried at all; they were right there, waiting to be stirred back up.

And deep down, a little voice whispered:

Can I really just be his friend?

Chapter 8

Myles Parker had always been the type of man who set his sights high and worked relentlessly to achieve his goals. When he first met Shonda Peterson during undergrad, he knew almost instantly she was out of his league. She was everything: smart, driven, effortlessly beautiful, and carrying an air of confidence that intimidated most men. But Myles wasn't most men.

Shonda, however, didn't make it easy for him.

"Sorry, I don't have time for distractions," she'd said with a sly smile the first time he asked her out after one of their shared study sessions in the library.

"Who said anything about distractions? I'm trying to be an addition," Myles quipped back, flashing the same confident grin that would eventually become one of his trademarks.

She rolled her eyes, but the corners of her mouth twitched with the hint of a smile. Myles had a charm that was hard to resist, even for someone as headstrong as Shonda.

For the next six months, Myles showed her exactly how serious he was. He walked her to class, carried her books, and sat through campus club meetings he had no interest in, all just to spend time with her. His patience and persistence eventually wore down her resolve, and she agreed to their first date, a modest outing at a burger joint off campus.

That night, over milkshakes and fries, they talked for hours about their dreams and fears. Shonda confessed her ambitions of becoming a criminal defense attorney and starting her own nonprofit for underprivileged youth. Myles shared his vision of building a life where he could take care of his family and leave a legacy.

By the end of the evening, Shonda realized that Myles wasn't just another college boy looking for a fling. He was someone with depth, ambition, and integrity. It didn't take long for her to fall for him, too.

After graduation, Myles proposed in front of their closest friends and family. Shonda said yes through tears of joy, and they married the following year.

The first three years of their marriage were pure bliss. Myles landed a coveted associate position at a prestigious consulting law firm, while Shonda secured a job at a leading criminal defense law firm. They were the picture-perfect power couple, two young professionals on the rise, deeply in love, and fiercely supportive of each other's goals.

They spent weekends traveling, hosting dinner parties, and daydreaming about the future. Myles often marveled at how lucky he was to have Shonda by his side. "I hit the jackpot," he'd tell anyone who would listen.

But beneath the surface, small cracks were beginning to form. By their fourth year of marriage, Myles's career demands intensified. He was putting in twelve-hour days at the firm, sometimes more, and often brought work home with him. He justified it by telling himself, and Shonda, that he was building their future.

"You'll see," he'd say. "Once I make partner, things will settle down. It's all for us."

But Shonda wasn't convinced.

At first, she tried to be understanding. She knew Myles's ambition was one of the things she loved about him. But as the months went on, she started to feel like an afterthought. Myles would come home late, too tired to hold a conversation, let alone notice the effort she put into their home and their relationship.

Date nights became rare, replaced by nights where Myles fell asleep on the couch with his laptop open. Shonda tried to express her frustrations, but Myles didn't seem to hear her. "I'm doing this for us," he'd repeat, as though that explanation absolved him of everything else.

Her resentment grew.

By the middle of year four, things between them had become tense. Shonda started to act out in small, passive-aggressive ways. She'd leave for work without saying goodbye, decline his calls during the day, and pick fights over trivial things like the way he folded the laundry or the toothpaste cap being left off.

Myles, ever the peacemaker, didn't argue back. He thought giving her space and keeping his head down at work would fix things. He believed that once he achieved his career goals, they'd find their way back to each other.

But Shonda didn't see it that way.

She began volunteering for overnight and out-of-town assignments more frequently, leaving Myles alone in their spacious suburban home. At first, he chalked it up to her needing a break from him. But as time went on, her absences became more noticeable.

Myles stood in the doorway of their bedroom, suit jacket slung over his shoulder, expression tight. "We need to talk."

Shonda didn't look up from her mirror. She was applying lipstick, slowly and deliberately, as if he hadn't just dropped five words heavy enough to shift the air.

"Oh?" she replied casually. "About what?"

He stepped farther into the room, dropping his jacket onto the chair. "Don't do that. You know what."

Shonda finally turned, arching an eyebrow. "You've been in your feelings ever since I went out with the girls last weekend. What's going on, Myles? You jealous now?"

"I'm not stupid, Shonda." His voice was low and controlled. "You've been distant for months. Coming home late. Always on your phone. You look at me like I'm an inconvenience, not your husband."

She scoffed, standing to face him. "Wow. So now I'm cheating because I have a social life and don't revolve around your schedule?"

"I didn't say you were cheating," he replied carefully. "But something's not right. I feel it. And I need you to be real with me."

Shonda folded her arms, eyes narrowing. "Or maybe you feel guilty. Maybe you're just projecting because you've been absent the majority of our marriage. You've missed anniversaries, birthdays, and my promotion celebration. Now suddenly you want to point fingers?"

Myles swallowed hard. The words hit like they were meant to, because they were true. No matter how much he wished he could take back those nights he devoted to climbing the corporate ladder, he couldn't, and this was his consequence. Shonda was right.

"I know I wasn't perfect," he said, voice thick. "I know I buried myself in work. I've apologized for that, and I've tried to change. But this... this callousness? That's not you. Not the woman I married."

Shonda turned away, her posture a little too still.

He stepped closer. "I'm asking you one last time. If you are honest, we could possibly get past this. I can feel something is wrong, but you have to tell me if we are going to be able to get through this. Are you seeing someone else?"

She glanced back over her shoulder, her face unreadable. "No. You're just paranoid."

He nodded slowly, lips pressed together. Everything in him screamed she was lying. The way she couldn't meet his eyes. The way her voice clipped at the end. The way the air between them felt hollow.

But he had no proof. Just a gut feeling, and the slow ache of his heart breaking in real time.

"Okay," he said finally, his voice quiet. "If that's your story."

Shonda didn't respond.

He grabbed his keys from the nightstand, not trusting himself to say anything more without exploding.

As he walked out, her perfume lingered in the hall, sickly sweet and sharp like the lie he couldn't prove but couldn't ignore.

A month had passed since Myles and Shonda's stand-off, and she had been just as distant. Myles worked extra hard to prove he was present and still wanted his marriage despite the changes in his wife. After a long day, Myles was headed out of the office when the other partners invited him out for drinks. Myles, knowing he was in for more of Shonda's resentful behavior at home, agreed to join them.

The bar at the fancy hotel downtown shimmered with gold accents and polished marble, the low murmur of conversation blending with jazz spilling from the grand piano in the corner. Myles nursed his whiskey, half listening to the senior partners at his firm swap stories and drop names like confetti.

It should've been a good night, a celebration. They were talking about Atlanta expansion again, tossing around his name with phrases like lead counsel and regional office head. But the words felt like static in his ears.

He savored his drink, his eyes drifting to the lobby as the elevator doors opened with a soft chime.

And then his entire body stilled.

There she was. He rubbed his eyes because he could not believe it. He blinked three times for good measure. He had to make sure it wasn't a mirage, that he was not, in fact, so tired he was seeing things.

It was Shonda. It was no mistake. That beautiful woman was indeed his wife. She descended from the elevator in a deep plum dress that clung to her curves like it had been poured on. Her hand was linked with someone else's. Jahlil. The coworker she always swore was *just a friend.* The one she casually teased him about being jealous of.

They were laughing. Intimate. Too close.

Myles's stomach twisted.

He fumbled for his phone and snapped a picture, his hands trembling slightly, but steady enough to capture the truth. The kind of truth that couldn't be dodged or explained away. Evidence he needed to confront her.

He stood, smoothing the front of his suit with forced calm. "I'm going to step out for a second," he murmured to the group. No one looked up.

Slipping away from the bar, he followed at a distance, heart pounding like a war drum. Shonda and Jahlil moved toward the hotel's main exit, stopping just inside the glass double doors. She wrapped both arms around his waist, leaning in like she couldn't bear to let go.

Myles stopped a few feet back, half-shielded by a marble column. Watching.

Jahlil cupped her face, kissing her as if she were his lifeline, as if he'd vowed to love and cherish her before God.

Shonda melted into him in response.

The kind of response Myles hadn't received in years.

His throat burned. Rage, heartbreak, disbelief, every emotion tangled together in his chest, sharp and heavy.

With trembling fingers, he dialed her number. Across the lobby, he watched her glance at her phone, see his name, and... roll her eyes.

She declined the call.

Then tipped her chin back up and kissed Jahlil again, deeper this time, one hand in his curls, the other resting possessively on his chest.

Myles stood in the shadows, frozen.

That was it.

No more denial or second-guessing. No more lying to himself.

His wife was gone.

Myles drove around for what felt like hours, trying to decompress and mentally prepare himself to confront Shonda. His hands gripped the steering wheel like it was the only thing tethering him to Earth. Rage, betrayal, and heartbreak churned in his chest like a storm.

When he finally arrived home, he didn't waste a second.

Shonda was already out of her clothes and in her pajamas, lounging on the couch like it was any other night. Myles stepped inside, his eyes locked on her.

"I loved seeing you in that purple dress," he said calmly, though his voice was tight. "It's always been my favorite on you."

Shonda froze. She hadn't seen Myles while wearing that dress. She'd changed before she left work to go celebrate with Jahlil.

Myles stepped closer, his tone still eerily calm. "I gave you the opportunity to come clean. I was willing to put it all behind us if you had just been honest with me."

Shonda sat in silence, shame tightening her features. She couldn't find a single word in her defense.

"And on top of everything, it was Jahlil?" Myles scoffed, his voice cracking with disbelief. "You gaslit me for years, made me feel like I was paranoid. You teased me about being jealous, made me out to be insecure. The whole time, you were fucking him."

He rarely used that kind of language with her, but the fury inside him needed a release. Words were all he had in this moment, and they were safer than anything else he might've done.

The expletive snapped Shonda out of her silence. Her expression shifted, eyes narrowing with a blaze of anger.

"Yes. Yes, I fucked him," she spat. "Tonight, we were actually celebrating our new family."

Myles's face turned to stone. His chest tightened, and he struggled to breathe. He didn't move.

Shonda kept going, her voice hard and bitter. "You were too busy to be a husband, let alone a father. You bought this big ass house and filled it with nothing but lonely memories. I'm tired, Myles. I sat here for years, neglected and forgotten, while you chased ambition. I found a man who can do both."

Myles turned away, refusing to let her see the tears threatening to fall. His hand gripped the doorknob. Just before he opened it, he glanced back over his shoulder.

"My lawyer will contact you tomorrow morning," he said coldly. "Have all your shit out of my house by the end of the week."

Without another word, he walked out, before the rage and heartbreak inside him did something unforgivable.

His marriage was over.

And it had ended with the most crushing blow of his life.

Chapter 9

I never planned to stay in this Airbnb for more than a week. It was supposed to be a temporary escape, enough time for Shonda to pack her shit, and get out of our home. I couldn't stand to be near her, not after what I saw.

The image of her wrapped around Jahlil like he was her everything, like I was not the one she made those vows to, still burned behind my eyes. That purple dress. That smug little smile. Her hand in his.

My attorney did exactly what I asked and contacted her the next morning. I wanted it formal. No back and forth, no arguing, just business. Just the facts: she had a week to vacate. We were starting divorce proceedings, and I needed my space.

But when my lawyer called me back two days later, his tone already said what I didn't want to hear.

"She's refusing to leave the home."

I blinked, the words settling like a weight on my chest. "Refusing?"

"She said, and I'm quoting, 'That house is just as much mine as it is his.'"

I laughed. Cold. Bitter. "So what now?"

"There's not much we can do yet," he said carefully. "Unfortunately, until assets are divided, she's not legally required to leave. It'll have to be settled through the divorce."

I thanked him and hung up, my hands shaking with a fury I hadn't felt in years. She knew exactly what she was doing. She wanted to hold on to the last piece of leverage she had. The house I bought. The one I worked night and day to pay for.

I didn't confront her. Not right away. I gave it time, a week or two. I told myself I needed to cool down, to think logically, not emotionally. But no matter how many workouts I powered through or how many times I paced the length of that rental house, I couldn't shake it.

I couldn't sleep. Every time I closed my eyes, I saw her. With him. In our bed. In our kitchen. Pregnant, glowing, laughing. Making memories with him that were supposed to be ours.

I hated that I missed her. That I still loved the idea of her, the version of her that I thought was real.

When I thought I was ready, I called.

I didn't even give her time to say hello.

"How dare you try to keep the house I bought?" I snapped.

There was a pause.

Then she calmly corrected me.

"We bought."

That made my blood boil.

Shonda launched a vicious verbal attack. "I earned that house," she spat. "Every lonely night I spent waiting for your ass to come home. Every missed dinner, every court case you dragged into our bed instead of intimacy and passion. I paid for that house in tears and disappointments. This was my dream house," she said, her voice sharp. "The one I picked out to raise my children in. The only part of that plan that changed was you. I'm raising this baby, my baby, in my house."

I felt like I'd been slapped.

Shonda wasn't finished. "If you're nice, I'll buy you out. If not, I'll see you in court."

The line went dead.

I stared at the phone, my whole body shaking. My jaw clenched, so hard it ached. How could she say that, so casually? How could she be so cruel and uncaring? Had she never loved me at all? How could she talk to me like I hadn't tried to give her everything? Like I didn't matter.

I was still standing there, fuming, torn between crying like a baby and punching a hole through these people's wall when my phone vibrated again.

It was as if the Lord himself knew I needed an out.

And just like that, the night took a better turn.

Lani had texted me, asking how I was holding up and if I wanted to grab lunch the next day.

That simple message broke through the weight pressing down on me like sunlight cutting through fog.

In that exact moment, the darkness I thought might swallow me whole... vanished. Just like that. As if it had never even existed.

She had that kind of presence.

Even in the middle of my anger, heartbreak, and the wreckage of everything I thought I knew, I could still feel her light. And somehow, that light always found its way to me.

It hit me hard. Clear and honest like a horse kick to the chest.

Lani had to be in my life. In some capacity, be that just a friend or the love of my life.

Whatever this was, whatever we were becoming, I wasn't letting it go. I would nurture it until it blossomed into whatever the universe meant for us to be.

Chapter 10

Over the next few weeks, Myles and I fell into a rhythm. It wasn't exactly normal. What even is normal after everything we've both been through? It was, however, comfortable. We just had a natural ebb and flow between us. Our conversations were a mix of playful banter, teasing jabs, and surprisingly deep dives into topics I'd never shared with anyone else but Sean. Lunches at Reel Catch, late-night texts when he couldn't sleep, and even a few brief phone calls while I was stuck in traffic.

It felt easy. Almost too easy.

One Friday afternoon, we met for lunch at this trendy little lunch spot downtown. Myles got there first of course. He always did, and snagged a table near the window. He waved me over as soon as I walked in, and I caught the way his eyes lit up when he saw me. I was wearing this flowy mustard-colored dress, and I guess it made an impression because his gaze lingered way too long.

"Fashionably late, as always," he teased as I slid into the seat across from him.

I smirked and rolled my eyes. "I'm not late. You're just early. Big difference."

That's how our lunches always felt, comfortable, like we'd known each other for years. But that day... something felt off. Maybe it was the way he kept brushing my hand when he laughed, or how his compliments seemed a little more charged than usual. I couldn't quite put my finger on it, but I felt the shift.

"So," he said, setting down his fork after finishing his salad. "What's next for you? Any big plans?"

I shrugged, stirring the last bit of my iced tea with my straw. "Just work. I've got another collaboration next week, but nothing too exciting. How about you?"

"I don't have anything interesting, really. I finally picked an apartment. I move in next week, so lots of unpacking. Nothing that compares to yours. You make everything sound so interesting," his tone soft and reflective.

I raised an eyebrow. "Do I?"

"I mean it," he said, leaning forward a bit. "You have this way of... I don't know. Making people feel like they're part of something special."

I froze, my hand tightening around my glass. "Myles..."

He seemed to catch himself, his eyes widened like he realized he'd just stepped over a line. "Sorry," he said quickly, leaning back in his chair. "I didn't mean to make things weird."

But the air between us had already shifted. The line had been crossed, even if only for a moment.

On the walk back to my car, I knew I couldn't leave things hanging. "Myles, we need to talk."

He stopped, hands in his pockets, watching me with that same awareness that made it hard to be mad, but I pushed through it.

"I need you to understand something," I said, carefully choosing my words. "I like you. I value our friendship. But that's all it can be. You're in the middle of a divorce, and I... I just can't be that person for you. I'm seeing someone. It's still new, but it has potential. I don't want to give either of you the wrong impression. I cannot offer you anything other than friendship. Can you handle that boundary?"

He nodded, his expression serious. "I'm sorry I got a little ahead of myself in there. I fully understand where you're coming from."

"Do you?" I asked, firmer this time. "Because if you can't respect that boundary, then we need to stop this now."

"I respect it," he said, his voice steady. "I swear, Lani. I just… got caught up in the moment. It won't happen again."

I studied him for a moment. "Good. Because I'm serious, Myles. I can't go down that road with you. I'm not that type of woman. I'm loyal, sometimes even to a fault. There is no room for infidelity with me. You of all people should appreciate that. I am willing to be your friend. If you need someone to vent to, I am your girl. But that is all. Take it from me, someone who has suffered one of the hardest betrayals ever, take this time, to heal. You are a good man, but in order to keep it that way, you are going to have to heal, and that is a journey you have to take on your own."

He flinched, just barely, but I saw it. His eyes then softened as if he was just registering what I said. As if he were taking a mental note to revisit my revelation at a different time. Luckily, he didn't say anything else. I had no desire to relive my trauma in this moment.

We said our goodbyes and went our separate ways, the awkward tension still clinging to me, stifling like humid summer air.

A couple nights later, Sean came over for a much-needed girls' night. She showed up like the hero she always was, with two bottles of wine and a bag full of snacks.

"Tonight," she declared, "we're solving all of our problems, one glass at a time."

We curled up on the couch, surrounded by chips, chocolate, and an absurd amount of cheese. I didn't waste any time diving into the awkward lunch incident. Sean's eyebrows shot up when I got to the part where I laid down the law with Myles. "Girl, you really laid it on thick, huh?"

"I had to," I said, taking a long sip of wine. "He was getting too comfortable. And I can't do that, Sean. Not with everything he's going through."

She nodded thoughtfully, rocking her glass. "I get it. But are you sure you're not catching feelings?"

I gave her a look. "Don't even start."

"I'm just saying!" she said, raising her hands in surrender. "You two clearly have chemistry. But I get why you're cautious. You're smart to protect yourself."

I sighed and leaned back. "It's not just about protecting myself. It's about protecting him too. He needs to figure out his life before trying to pull someone else into it. I'm afraid he'll end up leaning on me for emotional support instead of standing on his own two feet. And if he wants to be good for someone after this divorce, that's the work he has to do."

Sean gave me a serious nod. "Fair point. But for the record? You handled it well. Firm, but fair. Very grown woman energy."

We both laughed, the tension starting to melt. I updated her on my latest dates with Darius, including the one at the art studio.

"He had us painting and making pottery like we were in Ghost, or something," I said, rolling my eyes. "But I'll admit, it was... sweet. And the wine didn't hurt. There was a moment though that was very odd. The instructor called him Mr. Price, but his name is McRay, so I don't know what that was about. Darius just corrected her and kept it moving, but her body language said she was still confused."

Sean tilted her head. "Okay, weird. Other than the name thing, how is he? Is he giving what he's supposed to give?"

I hesitated. Darius's smile, his laugh, the way he paid attention to the little things I said, all of it replayed in my mind. "He's great. Really great. But..."

"But?" she asked, leaning in.

"I don't know. I like him. A lot. But I feel like I'm holding back, and I don't know why."

Sean tilted her head, studying me. "You think it has anything to do with Myles?"

I groaned and buried my face in my hands. "Why does everything have to come back to him?"

"Because you two have unfinished business! I saw that connection, and that cannot be faked. It was the most obvious thing in the world," she said.

I sighed and reached for my wine. "I don't want unfinished business. I want clarity. Simplicity."

"Don't we all," Sean said with a chuckle.

We talked more as the wine flowed, loosening our tongues and shifting into that awkward space where girl talk turns into complaining about how much we love and hate men.

"Why are men so... complicated?" I asked. I lifted my glass to my nose, savoring the notes of cherry, rose, and cedar.

"Because they're men," Sean replied with a shrug. "It's in their DNA."

I laughed and shook my head. "I just feel like I'm constantly trying to figure them out. It's exhausting."

Sean lifted her glass. "Here's to the men who keep us guessing, and to the wine that makes it bearable."

We clinked glasses, laughing until we were breathless.

"Seriously though," she said, reaching over to squeeze my hand. "You're handling this better than I would. Between Myles and Darius, I'd have lost my mind."

"Trust me," I said with a dry smile. "I'm close. But I'm trying. That's all I can do."

"And you're doing great, babe. Don't let anyone tell you otherwise. You've drawn clear boundaries, and you've stuck to them. Personally, I would have already ridden that ride, because that man is fine, and I know you've got cobwebs between those thighs." She laughed, and I rolled my eyes.

As midnight rolled around, my phone buzzed with a message. I glanced at the screen, and my heart skipped a beat.

Darius: Thinking about you. Hope you had a good day. Can't wait to see you again soon.

Sean peeked over my shoulder and grinned. "Looks like someone's got it bad."

I smiled, my cheeks warm. "Maybe."

But as I set my phone down, a thought crept into my mind, one I couldn't shake, no matter how hard I tried.

Why did it feel like things were about to get a whole lot more complicated?

Chapter 11

I was on cloud nine. Sean's birthday bash was a whirlwind. There was laughter, music, and cocktails. I'd lost count of how many shots we'd taken, but I remembered the warmth of our toast: to friendship, to growth, to leaving drama behind. I left the club feeling light, a little unsteady on my feet, but genuinely happy.

That feeling disappeared the moment I stepped through my front door.

My breath caught in my throat as I took in the chaos. My usually tidy living room was a disaster. Couch cushions were ripped open, my coffee table was flipped on its side, and books were strewn across the floor.

But the worst part was my bedroom.

I walked in hesitantly, my heart pounding in my chest. Drawers were yanked open, their contents dumped onto the floor. Even my most intimate belongings, my lingerie, keepsakes, and private journals, had been tossed carelessly, like trash.

I felt exposed, violated in a way I couldn't even describe.

Tears welled up in my eyes as I fumbled for my phone and dialed the police.

They arrived quickly. Their presence was both reassuring and overwhelming. I answered their questions as best I could, though my voice shook with every word.

"No, nothing of value seems to be missing," I said, glancing around the room. "But... everything is just," My voice broke, and I gestured helplessly at the mess around me.

The officers took notes and promised to do what they could, but their words felt hollow. After they left, I sat on the couch, now awkwardly upright again, and stared blankly at the wreckage.

My next instinct was to call someone who would make me feel safe. Without thinking, I dialed Darius.

"Lani?" His voice was groggy but instantly concerned. "What's wrong?"

I sniffled, my voice trembling. "Someone broke into my apartment. It's a mess. I don't know what to do."

"I'm coming over," he said immediately.

"No, you don't have to."

"Lani," he interrupted firmly. "I'm coming. Don't argue."

Fifteen minutes later, Darius was at my door, still in sweats and a hoodie. The sight of him made me burst into tears all over again.

"Hey, hey," he said softly, pulling me into his arms. "It's okay. I've got you."

The warmth of his embrace, and the steady rhythm of his heartbeat against my cheek calmed me in a way I hadn't expected.

He stayed the night, insisting on sleeping on the couch even though I tried to argue. I was too drained to put up much of a fight, collapsing into bed after triple-checking that the front door was locked.

By morning, Darius had a plan.

"You need cameras and an alarm system," he said over coffee.

"Darius, that's expensive," I replied, shaking my head. "I'm not exactly rolling in money."

"I don't care," he said simply. "Your safety isn't up for debate."

Before I could argue further, he had already pulled up a website on his phone, scrolling through top-rated security systems.

I watched in awe as he not only purchased a full system for me but spent hours setting it up. He installed cameras at the front and back entrances, mounted sensors on the windows, and even tested the alarm to make sure it worked properly.

"Why are you doing all this?" I asked quietly, watching him drill a camera mount into place.

He paused, looking at me with an expression that was both earnest and tender. "Because I care about you, Lani. And because you deserve to feel safe in your own home. Not to mention, I can't be here 24 hours a day as much as I would like to be. You need to feel safe, and I also need peace of mind."

My heart swelled, and for a moment, I couldn't find the words to respond. I had never felt protected like this before. The feeling was indescribable.

By the time Darius was done, my apartment felt like a fortress. But even with the new security measures in place, I couldn't shake the unease that lingered in the air.

"Why would someone break in and not take anything?" I mused aloud. "It doesn't make sense."

Darius frowned, his arms crossed as he leaned against the kitchen counter. "Are you sure nothing's missing? Nothing at all?"

"Nothing valuable," I said, shaking my head. "At least, not that I've noticed."

"Maybe it wasn't about stealing," he said, his voice low.

My stomach twisted at the implication. I didn't want to think about what that might mean.

As the day wore on, I found myself watching Darius more closely. The way he moved, the way he spoke, the way he seemed to care so deeply, it all felt surreal. He was, quite literally, my knight in shining armor. But that scared me.

I wasn't used to being taken care of like this. And as much as I appreciated everything Darius had done for me, I couldn't help but wonder if I was ready for someone like him. Or what this care would cost me in the long run.

That night, after Darius left, I sat on the couch, staring at the newly installed monitor that displayed the camera feeds. I felt safer, but not entirely at ease.

My phone buzzed with a message.

Darius: Let me know if you need anything else. I'll be there in a heartbeat.

I smiled, my fingers hovering over the keyboard as I tried to think of how to respond.

Finally, I typed back:

Me: Thank you for everything, Darius. I don't know what I'd do without you.

But even as I hit send, a part of me couldn't stop questioning why my heart still felt so uneasy.

Chapter 12

She's slipping.

I can feel it.

Lani... she's too comfortable. Too damn confident. Independent to a fault. She's moving like she doesn't need me, like I'm some accessory to her perfect little life, something she can take or leave. And that? That's a problem.

She's supposed to need me. Not just want me, need me. Wake up thinking about me kind of need. Call me for everything kind of need. But that's not her. Not yet. Not like I need her.

She goes hours, sometimes a full day, without texting. Does she know what that does to me? Does she know how it burns to be left on read when all I do is think about her? Watch her? Plan for her?

She should be grateful someone like me sees her. Understands her. A man who is willing to give up everything for her.

And now this, Sean's birthday party. Everyone was there. Everyone, but me. No invite. Not even a heads-up. Just pictures online, tagged, smiling, like she didn't even consider how that would look. Like she wasn't mine.

That's what set it off.

If she won't let me in... I'll make her need me. She thinks she's so secure in her little apartment. Her own space. Her sanctuary with her own rules. Her boundaries. But what happens when that security is shattered? When the one place she feels safe suddenly isn't?

What happens when someone breaks in, rummages through her things, just enough to scare her?

Not enough to hurt her. Never that. I'd never hurt her. But scare her? Shake her? Yeah. Yeah, maybe she needs that. Then I can come in. Play the hero. Comfort her. Offer to help, really help. Like, "let me install cameras" help. Top-of-the-line security, all the bells and whistles. I already know which ones to use. Discreet. Reliable. Night vision. Audio. She won't question it. Not when she's scared.

Not when she's vulnerable.

And when those cameras are in… I'll finally see everything. Every move. Every person. Every moment.

It's not about control. It's about closeness. She doesn't let me close, not in the way I need. So I'll make the way.

This isn't crazy. This is love.

Sometimes love just needs a little push.

And after this? She'll see. She'll realize I'm the only one who truly has her back.

Not Sean. Not Carlos. Not any of those vultures she surrounds herself with.

Me.

Always me.

The weeks after the break-in were a blur. What started as a horrifying invasion of my personal space seemed to ripple through every corner of my life. I found myself double-checking the locks and glancing over my shoulder in parking lots. Even inside my own apartment, now secured with a top-of-the-line system, I couldn't shake the unease. To my surprise, Darius seemed just as affected. His protective instincts kicked into overdrive. He was always there, checking in with a text, calling just to see how I was doing.

"Did you make it home safe?"

"Did you sleep okay?"

"What's for dinner tonight? Want me to bring something?"

At first, it was sweet. He was going above and beyond to make me feel safe, and I appreciated it. But as the days turned into weeks, his constant presence started to feel... heavy. Stifling. Irritating as hell.

This morning started off badly, and only got worse. I had planned to bake cookies for an upcoming event, a task I could usually do in my sleep. Somehow, I managed to burn not just one, but two batches.

Frustrated, I turned my attention to filming content, only for my camera to die halfway through. When I checked my bag for the backup battery, I remembered I'd left it at Sean's after our last wine night. And then, an email popped up. A custom order I'd promised to finish by the end of the week. Now I'd have to pull an all-nighter just to stay on track.

By the time Darius called, I was already stretched thin.

"Hey, beautiful," he greeted me cheerfully.

I pressed the phone to my ear while scrubbing a scorched cookie sheet. "Hey," I replied, trying to keep my voice neutral.

"You sound stressed. What's going on?"

"It's just been one of those days," I said with a sigh. "Everything that could go wrong, did."

"Well, I can come over," he offered quickly. "Let me take care of you tonight. I'll bring dinner, we can watch a movie."

"Darius," I interrupted, a little sharper than I meant to.

There was a pause. "Yeah?"

I took a breath, trying to rein it in. "I appreciate everything you've done these past few weeks. I really do. But I need to be honest with you."

"Okay," he said slowly.

"I feel like... like you're smothering me," I said before I could stop myself. "It's like you're always there, always texting, always calling. I barely have a moment to breathe."

Another pause. "I thought you liked that I was attentive," he said, his voice suddenly quieter.

I could be wrong, but it sounded like he said it through clenched teeth? I just glossed over that, because it was more than likely just me being sensitive in this moment, projecting my own feelings.

"I did," I said quickly. "But it's too much now. I need some space."

He went silent for a beat, and I wondered if he'd hung up. Then he finally said, "I didn't realize I was making you feel that way. I just wanted to be there for you."

"I know, and I'm thankful. But I need to feel like myself again. I need to find balance. This experience has shifted something in me, and I'm afraid I'll start relying too much on you for my safety when I need to be okay on my own. I've worked hard to be self-sufficient, and I need to get back to that."

"I see," he said, but there was something in his tone, tight and clipped, that made my stomach twist.

"This isn't about not liking you, or not wanting you around," I added quickly. "I just… I need to set some boundaries. For my own sanity."

"Boundaries," he repeated like he was testing the word out loud.

"Yes."

There was another long silence before he finally said, "Okay, Lani. If that's what you need, I'll respect it."

I let out a breath I hadn't even realized I was holding. "Thank you."

When the call ended, I felt a strange mixture of relief and guilt. I hated confrontation, and the conversation left me emotionally drained. But even though I appreciated Darius's support, I couldn't deny the weight that lifted now that I'd spoken up.

Still… something about his reaction unsettled me. His words were understanding, but his tone had shifted, just slightly, enough to make me wonder.

"Maybe I'm overthinking it," I murmured, pushing the thought aside.

Chapter 14

Boundaries?

I sat in my car, fingers clenched around the steering wheel until my knuckles went pale. That word echoed over and over again like a slap I couldn't dodge.

She wanted space.

I replayed the call in my head, hearing the way her voice trembled with discomfort. Not fear. Discomfort, with me. After everything I'd done. After all the time I spent making sure she felt safe, protected, cared for.

This is how she repaid me?

I gave her everything, my time, my energy, my focus. I dropped my own life to support hers. And now she wants to "feel like herself again?" As if my presence is a burden?

No.

No, no, no.

A shadow crept up behind my eyes, one I'd tried to push down ever since the break-in. I thought it would fade once she leaned into me, once she saw how deeply I could love her.

But now? Now I realized something far worse.

What if she doesn't need me anymore?

The thought made my chest burn. The kind of burn that scorched. I popped open my laptop and logged into her security feed. I told her the system was state-of-the-art, and it was.

Because I made sure it was. I designed every camera placement, every login credential.

Watching her had become part of my routine. Like brushing my teeth. Like breathing.

But tonight, it wasn't enough to just watch.

Tonight, I was planning.

If she thought she could push me away by telling me she needs space, she was wrong. I wasn't going anywhere. I'd sacrificed too much, invested too much.

She said she needed space?

Fine. I'd give her the illusion of it. Let her think she was in control. Let her breathe. But we are in this for the long haul, there's no such thing as space. She doesn't understand it yet, but it's me and her forever.

I'm still going to be right here, just out of frame.

Because Lani was mine.

And no one, not even her, was going to take that away from me.

Chapter 15

Darius had been surprisingly easygoing ever since I asked for space. I half expected pushback or guilt trips, but instead he responded with a simple, "I understand, beautiful. Take all the time you need."

And yet… he didn't disappear.

He sent the occasional "thinking of you" text, funny memes about dating woes, and links to local art events he thought I might enjoy. It was just enough to keep him in my periphery without overwhelming me. I really appreciated that about him.

After a couple of weeks, I agreed to dinner.

We met at a small, upscale jazz lounge tucked into the city's art district. Darius had remembered that I loved live performances, especially the soulful, melodic kind that stirred raw emotion. I loved to feel my music as much as I listened to it, like a balm to my soul.

"You look amazing," he said when I arrived, his eyes drinking me in like he hadn't seen me in years.

He kissed my cheek lightly, then offered his arm.

Inside, the lighting was warm and low, the music just loud enough to allow conversation. Darius was funny that night, charming, attentive, making me laugh in a way that eased the weight of the past few weeks. When he was in his element like this, I could see myself building a life with him.

But there were moments.

He'd mention something I hadn't told him. A comment about a new blouse I was wearing that I'd only posted in a quick story. A reference to the fact I'd been at the nail salon that afternoon, even though I hadn't shared that publicly.

"Are you psychic?" I teased, half joking, watching his face closely.

He only smiled. "Let's just say I like keeping up with the people I care about."

The band launched into a slow number, and Darius reached for my hand. "Dance with me."

We moved slowly, swaying to the music. It should've been romantic, perfect even. But for just a second, when I looked into his eyes, it felt like something was off. He looked… possessive, not in an overtly creepy way, but like he was imagining something far more serious than I was at this moment.

Still, I brushed it off.

A few days later, Darius surprised me with a private couples cooking class.

"I remembered you said you wanted to get better at making Thai food," he said, grinning. "Figured we could both learn something."

The studio kitchen was charming, with warm wood tones, mason jars filled with spices, and the soft scent of lemongrass already hanging in the air. It made me smile that he remembered such a small, random detail. I don't exactly remember telling him this, but I told myself to relax and just enjoy the moment. I had prayed for a man who would love me out loud, someone who paid attention to the little things, and made me feel seen. Darius was doing all of that, so why did this nagging feeling still linger, keeping me from fully committing or taking things further? Sean swears it's because Myles is still in the picture, but deep down, I think it's something else.

The night went well. We laughed through failed spring rolls, flirted as we plated curry, and shared wine between tasks. Darius was in his element, confident and smooth.

Still… there were just little things again. Nagging suspicions I found hard to ignore.

He seemed to know exactly where I kept my phone in my bag. He guessed my PIN when I handed it to him to take a picture.

"How'd you…"

"I watch you more than you think," he said, teasingly.

It came out as a joke, but my stomach dipped slightly.

Later, when we were back in my neighborhood, he insisted on walking me to my door. "You never know," he said. "People are crazy out here."

"You sound like Sean," I joked, unlocking my door.

Darius chuckled, but lingered a little too long at my threshold. His fingers brushed the door frame, as if marking it. "I'm glad we're doing this again."

I nodded, offering a soft smile. "Yeah… me too."

I didn't notice until I was getting ready for bed that my decorative towel had been moved. And I could've sworn I left my lipstick in the drawer, not on the counter.

But maybe I was just tired.

Maybe.

Still, as I crawled into bed, something in my gut pulled taut, like a violin string tuned too tight. I was about two seconds from asking my doctor about anxiety medication. The nervous unease never really let go, and I was starting to think something was very wrong with me.

I didn't want to say anything to Sean. Not yet. Not until I had something real, concrete. Right now I just have what feels like paranoia. If I brought this to my best friend, she would most definitely make me a tin hat and clown me.

Chapter 16

T he next morning, I sat at my kitchen table, cradling a mug of coffee, my thoughts spinning. I hadn't been sleeping well since the break-in. I had to make an appointment about the insomnia. Luckily, my doctor went ahead and prescribed something for me. Last night, I was just too consumed with the uneasy feeling to take it. Something about the way my lipstick had been left out, the towel folded differently in a new spot, the odd sense that someone else had been here, it wouldn't leave me alone. I found it extremely hard to feel safe mentally after the break-in. Even with all of the security equipment, I knew physically I was safe. If not safe, I was at least prepared. Mentally, though, I could not let my guard down, and it was exhausting. I would give it some more time though. I had not pulled out all my hair yet, so instead I did the next best thing.

I called Sean.

Ten minutes later, she showed up in leggings, and an Erykah Badu T-shirt with a matching head wrap, still rubbing the sleep from her eyes, and clutching an energy drink.

"You sounded off," she said, as she dropped onto the couch. "Talk to me."

I hesitated, suddenly unsure if I sounded as paranoid out loud as I did in my head.

"I know this is going to sound crazy..." I began. "But I think there's something funny going on with Darius."

Sean blinked. "Wait, what?"

"I don't know. But something's been feeling... off. Last night, after our date, I noticed things were moved. Little things. My lipstick, a towel in the bathroom. And earlier this week, he made a comment about where I keep my phone, and guessed my PIN."

She frowned, processing. "Okay. That's... odd. But maybe he saw your PIN when you typed it in? That kind of thing happens all the time."

I nodded slowly. "Yeah. That's what I thought. But then, he knew I went to the nail salon, and mentioned a top I wore in a story that was up for, like, ten minutes."

Sean leaned forward. "Girl, you do know you're an influencer, right? You put details of your life online for people to consume. Are you weirded out that he might have watched one of your stories? Really is that what we are doing? That's kind of the point, people watch. Maybe he's just observant."

"Too observant?"

"I mean... maybe he just likes you, and he's trying really hard not to screw it up. Especially since you asked for space. Maybe he's dialing it back, but still wants to be thoughtful."

I sighed, twisting my mug in my hands. "You're probably right. I just don't want to miss something important because I want it to be okay. After Michael, I'm trying really hard not to ignore red flags."

Sean's expression softened. "I get it. But you've been through hell. Your radar's going to be on high alert even when there's no threat. That's not crazy, it's survival. But you also don't want to sabotage something good out of fear."

I gave her a small smile. "You're the calm, sane voice in my head, you know that? Well, right now anyway, sometimes it's hard to tell whether you're the angel or the devil, but I appreciate you just the same."

"Yeah, well, the voice in your head needs another energy drink," Sean quipped, cracking hers open. "Keep your eyes open, but don't start building crime boards on your wall just yet, okay?"

I laughed, the tension easing just a little. But somewhere, deep in my gut, that taut string remained. No matter how much I wanted to will it away or pretend that it did not exist, the feeling still lingered.

Chapter 17

Damn it.

She noticed.

I was careful, no... meticulous. The candles, the pillows, the goddamn lingerie... everything went back the way I found it. I checked twice. Maybe three times. But that damn towel in the bathroom... I didn't angle it right. I had been too consumed by the feel, the smell of it...of her. To notice how it was placed in the bathroom. It was such an amateur move. I would have to do better next time. Then the lipstick...it was just calling my name from the drawer. I was caught in a spiral of imagining her rubbing it across those beautiful full lips. It just did something to me. I couldn't bear to put it back in the drawer, instead I left it on the counter. I should have taken it. Felt the sensation of rubbing it on me. Imagining the feeling of her lips instead.

Sloppy.

I just needed to consume more of her, faster. I felt as if I was going through withdrawals, so when I was finally in her space, I just wanted all of her at once. I have to do better.

I've been doing this long enough to know better. I should've been in and out. No lingering. No watching her sleep that extra five minutes from the hallway. No picking up her cardigan just to smell the scent she leaves behind. I let myself get... soft.

Now she's suspicious.

Not full-blown afraid, never that, but something's off in her. She looks at me like she's trying to connect dots. Like I've said something out of order, or like the pattern she built around me is cracking at the seams.

And it's infuriating.

Not because she's catching on.

Because I let her.

I gave her space. I played the good guy. The supportive boyfriend. I toned it down when she said she needed a breather, played it chill, laid back, even made her laugh on our date. I thought I was pulling it off.

But she still noticed.

She's slipping through my fingers, and it's not because I'm not good enough, it's because I got careless. All these months I've worked to be the version of me she wants, the man she can trust, lean on, come home to.

And I left a damn towel out of place.

She'll forgive herself for doubting me once I fix this. I'll give her something to feel safe about again. Rebuild the image. Patch the cracks.

But I swear to God... I won't make the same mistake twice.

Chapter 18

Life had grown quieter, simpler, for a while, at least. I spent most of my time pouring myself into my work, my hobbies, and my friendships, with only the occasional text or call from Myles to break the routine.

Myles's divorce, while progressing, had been anything but smooth. He and Shonda had agreed to part ways, both knowing there was no salvaging what they once had. But the house, their house, had become a point of contention.

It wasn't just property to them; it was a symbol of their shared dreams. More importantly, Myles had actually paid for the house, and the thought of his ex-wife raising her affair baby in it was a big HELL NO, and I did not blame him one bit. There is only so much you can expect from a man. He has feelings and emotions too, as much as we like to forget sometimes. Selling it was the only option left, but neither wanted to let it go. Still, the closing date had finally arrived, and I could tell the thought of it weighed heavily on Myles's mind.

I'd invited Myles over because I'd sensed his tension through our texts and calls over the last week. Though I'd kept a healthy distance to avoid any misunderstandings, I felt he could use a pick-me-up. Just to take his mind off everything that was going on, because I knew a change like this had to be hard for him.

When he arrived, I handed him a cold beer and gestured for him to sit on the couch.

"You look like you haven't slept in days," I said, sitting across from him.

"I haven't," he admitted, running a hand through his hair. "The house... I know it's just bricks and wood, but it feels like I'm losing a piece of myself. I worked so hard to buy that house for us to raise a family in. I can't help but feel anxious as I close this chapter. But I have to if I'm ever going to have the family I desperately want."

I nodded. "It's not just a house. I get it, but just because you and Shonda can't have the family you planned on doesn't mean it is out of the cards. Remember that healing I said you were going to need to do? This is the first step to building that life you want."

I took a breath, eyes distant as I spoke. "Michael, my ex, didn't just break my heart. He dismantled my spirit piece by piece. He used me, Myles. I paid his bills, cooked his meals, supported his dreams, and in return, he told me he was never attracted to me. That he had to force himself to touch me. He used to call me fat, say I should be grateful someone like him even looked my way. He told me no man would ever love me. And the worst part? I started to believe him. I stayed in that relationship far longer than I should have, hoping that if I just lost a little weight, loved him a little harder, bent a little more, he'd finally see me. But he never did. He used my body, my money, and my heart like they were disposable. I had to rebuild myself after that. I had to unlearn every lie he planted in me, and relearn how to love myself without condition.

I took my power back, Myles. And I swore I'd never give that kind of control to anyone again. I wasn't just healing from a breakup, I was healing from the way I stopped loving myself to keep someone else comfortable. I say all of that to say this. I came back from financial ruin, survived having my self-esteem and self-worth torn down to the studs. Yet I can still believe there is a love out there for me, you can survive this too, and thrive. It just takes work."

Myles went quiet for a minute while he processed what I had said.

When he did speak, he chose his words wisely. "First of all, he is an idiot. Not to make this awkward with the boundaries, but I have to say this. You are one of the most beautiful, stunning, charismatic women I have ever met in my life. Second, I am so glad you have healed, and you are still open to love. Snuffing out a light like yours is a great disservice to the world. You have brought me back from some dark times with just a simple text at the right moment. I cannot imagine anyone dimming your light on purpose. Third, what's his last name, so I can look him up and put him in his place?"

I giggled and playfully punched him in the arm.

We talked for over an hour, the conversation drifting from the house to lighter topics. For the first time in days, Myles laughed, a real, unburdened laugh that lit up his face.

Just as I was about to grab us another round of beers, the doorbell rang. I frowned, glancing at the clock. It was way too late for visitors, especially uninvited ones.

"Expecting anyone?" Myles asked.

"No," I said, my brow furrowing as I walked to the door.

When I opened it, my heart sank.

Darius stood there, his eyes wild and bloodshot, his chest heaving as though he'd run all the way to my apartment. His clothing was disheveled, and his fists were clenched tightly at his sides.

"Darius?" I said cautiously. "What are you doing here?"

He stepped inside without waiting for an invitation, his voice low and trembling with barely restrained anger. "What am I doing here? That's what you ask me? After everything I've done for you?"

"Darius, you need to leave," I said, my voice firm.

But he wasn't listening. His eyes darted past me to the living room, where Myles stood, beer in hand.

Darius's expression darkened. "Who the hell is this?"

My heart raced. "He's a friend. Darius, you're making a scene. Please leave."

"A friend?" Darius's voice rose. "You think I'm stupid? What kind of friend comes over this late to drink? You've been disrespecting me in our house?"

"Our house?" I repeated, confusion turning to panic. "This is my apartment, Darius. What are you even talking about?"

"I've sacrificed everything for you!" he shouted, stepping closer. "And this is how you repay me? By sneaking around with some other man?"

At that moment, Myles stepped into the doorway, his presence calm but commanding. "You need to leave, man. We are just friends, but regardless, you are making her uncomfortable, and she asked you to leave." He said, his voice steady.

Seeing Myles only seemed to push Darius further over the edge. Darius lunged.

The two men collided like freight trains, fists flying. Myles grunted as Darius caught him with a wild left hook, but he barely flinched. The adrenaline had kicked in.

Myles slammed his shoulder into Darius's chest, driving him into the wall. A picture frame shattered on impact.

Darius retaliated with a knee to Myles's side, then threw an elbow that grazed his temple. For a moment, I could tell Myles was a bit disoriented, but he bounced back.

He shook it off and grabbed Darius by the collar, landing two solid punches to the jaw. Darius stumbled back but recovered his footing almost immediately. He was fast, and fueled by rage.

"She's mine!" Darius screamed, diving again.

They crashed into the coffee table, splintering wood and sending remotes and coasters flying. Myles scrambled to his feet first, grabbed Darius by the back of the shirt, and slammed him face first into the wall.

"Are you serious right now? "Myles growled.

Darius roared, blood now trickling from his lip. He twisted free and rushed Myles like a bull.

Myles was ready.

He ducked low, drove a fist into Darius's ribs, and brought an uppercut straight to his chin. Darius's head snapped back, and he fell to one knee.

Panting, bleeding, shaking, he still tried to rise. Myles backed away, scanning the wrecked apartment. His eyes landed on a heavy metal lamp, thick base, cold steel neck.

"Bruh, I'm seriously not even trying to hurt you, right now, just stop!"

Darius rose slowly, sneering through bloodied teeth. "You think you are gonna come in and take..."

CRACK.

The lamp collided with the side of Darius's head. He dropped like a sack of bricks, dead weight, unconscious before he hit the floor.

I stared, wide-eyed, my hands trembling as I reached for my phone. "Oh my God, oh my God," I whispered.

"Call the police," Myles said, his voice calm as he bent down to check Darius's pulse. "He's breathing, but he needs medical attention and a 72-hour hold while they're at it."

The police arrived within minutes, followed by an ambulance. I explained everything, how Darius had shown up uninvited, his erratic behavior, and his attack on Myles.

The officers assured me that Darius would be charged with trespassing and assault, and that I could file for a restraining order which Myles said he would take care of.

As the EMT wheeled Darius out on a stretcher, he stirred briefly, his eyes fluttering open. His gaze locked on mine, and I shivered at the intensity of it.

"You think this is over?" he muttered, his voice slurred.

But it was over, or at least, I hoped it was.

When the police and EMTs finally left, the apartment was eerily quiet. I sat on the couch, staring at my hands.

Myles sat beside me, his hand lightly brushing mine. "You okay?" he asked softly.

I nodded, though my eyes brimmed with tears. "I didn't think he was capable of... any of this."

"Sometimes people hide who they really are," Myles said. "You did the right thing tonight."

I leaned into him, letting myself feel the weight of the night. For the first time in months, I had clarity. I finally understood that gnawing feeling I couldn't shake. The only question left was: What made him show up here? Did he know I had company? And if so... how?

Chapter 19

Pathetic.

That's what I am.

Laid out on her floor like some worthless intruder. Like I don't belong there. How can I protect her, if I couldn't even hold my own.

Weak.

Weak.

Weak.

He knocked me out. That smug bastard standing in our home, our sacred place, acting like I was the one who didn't have a right to be there.

And I let it slip.

Our home.

She wasn't ready to hear that. I let him… his presence knocked me off my square.

"God." I said it out loud.

She looked at me like I'd grown another head, like I'd shown her something she wasn't supposed to see yet. I've been so careful. I've played it calm, cool, supportive. I gave her room to breathe, space to feel safe. But it cracked. I cracked.

And all because of him. That pompous, self-righteous pretty boy strutting around like he's the goddamn hero. Myles. Her almost ex she's supposed to be past. A friend. And yet somehow, still in her apartment, in her head, in her life.

I saw the way she softened when she looked at him. I saw the hesitation, the doubt in me.

It made my stomach turn.

He thinks he's protecting her. But what does he know about her? About how she needs to be cared for, watched over, guided? She doesn't even realize how much she needs me. How much I've done to keep her safe.

And I let him walk away. Worse, I let him win. In front of her. I should've crushed his jaw, should've dragged him out by the throat like the disease he is.

Instead, I let him humiliate me.

That ends now.

I've spent too long trying to make her mine. To mold myself into the version she can trust, love, build a life with. But Myles... Myles is a threat to all of it. A parasite still clinging to her heart. And threats don't get negotiated with.

They get removed.

I can't just have her anymore.

I have to take her.

And to do that, I have to erase him. Permanently.

Chapter 20

Once things calmed down after Darius's episode, Sean came over to check on me, just to make sure I was fine and not too shaken up. Something about Darius showing up unannounced that night lingers in my mind like a splinter I can't remove. Every shadow seems darker now, every sound louder. For weeks, I haven't been able to shake the feeling that I'm being watched.

I finally voiced my fears to my best friend. We sat on my couch with glasses of wine, the TV murmuring in the background.

"I don't know if I'm being paranoid," I admitted, twisting the stem of my glass. "But it feels like Darius is watching me. Like I can't even relax in my own home."

Sean's playful expression vanished. "This started after Darius showed up, didn't it?"

I nodded.

She slammed her glass down. "I'd bet my left arm. If there is anything funny going on, it's that *security system* he installed. Let me call Carlos. He'll tear it apart and see what exactly is going on."

Carlos arrived the next evening with his laptop and a toolbox. As he hunched over my kitchen counter, typing furiously, I alternated between relief and dread.

"Gotta be honest," he said after an hour, "I thought Sean was exaggerating. But this?" He whistled. "This is intentional."

My stomach lurched. "What do you mean?"

He turned the screen toward me, his face grim. "Darius built a backdoor into your cameras. He's had access to every room, front door, living room, and bedroom. And judging by these logs? He's been watching regularly."

The room tilted. I gripped the counter to stay upright.

"Since the break-in," I whispered, the truth hitting like a sucker punch.

Sean shot up, knocking over her chair. "That sick bastard! He probably staged the break-in to get you to agree to install this shit!" She whirled to Carlos. "Baby I want to kick his ass. Even better can you erase him? Have him arrested? Do you know a guy? Something?"

Bile burned my throat. I barely made it to the bathroom before I threw up.

When I returned, Sean and Carlos were already ripping cameras from the walls.

"I cannot believe I was rooting for that sick bastard," Sean declared, before stomping the camera she had been holding.

By midnight, my apartment was littered with empty brackets and severed wires. Carlos was very thorough, even finding the cameras in my bedroom and throughout the house I did not know were there. The blank spots on the walls felt like fresh wounds, a visual representation of my trust in this moment.

I had let another man in that ended up being dangerous for me. In my defense, I was more aware this time. Sensing something was off, I never fully let my guard down.

Baby steps.

"I'm staying," Sean announced, tossing pillows onto the couch. "No arguments."

I was going to hire one of those high-tech security firms to come in and set up a state-of-the-art system when I realized I just had the best of the best in my living room. Sean called Carlos to send us over a shopping list for everything he would need to get me squared away.

"It's not cheap," Carlos warned after his inspection. "But I'll build you a fortress. Military-grade encryption, isolated network, zero room for back doors."

"Sounds like a plan to me," I said without blinking. I'm done cutting corners with my safety.

I let Darius come in with his fake sense of security, and he violated me, my trust, and my privacy. I was taking my power back over the situation. I was not a damsel in distress. I was a big girl with big-girl responsibilities. I can't lie and say it didn't hurt swiping that card though. Carlos must have thought he was setting up security for Beyoncé. But the peace of mind was worth it.

The security system was my first line of defense but Myles had become a steady presence, in contrast of Darius, a very appreciated presence.

Myles texted daily, but just a little short, *how are you feeling*, or *do you need anything*, text. He didn't make constant contact throughout the day. A nice quick visit here or there, dropping by with coffee or some other treat I might like if he was in the area. *I told him I was in.* Unlike Darius's suffocating obsession, Myles's care felt... natural.

Even though Myles and Darius's behavior was similar, it felt completely different. I think instinctively I could sense the difference between Darius's manufactured care and the genuine, more relaxed concern of Myles. His protectiveness was ingrained in him.

Even through all of this, he had been really laid back and chill. Not overbearing or fixated. Lately, though, there has been a new brightness to him. That was saying something, because Myles was the calmest and collected person I knew.

I loved what our friendship had grown into over the past few months. We shared everything: our accomplishments, our fears, even our goals. I felt safe with Myles. Safe enough to express my feelings, knowing I wouldn't be judged. I could tell that his mood shifted. It's like he had a purpose again.

"It's official," he told me yesterday, voice warm through the phone.

"The divorce?"

"Signed, and sealed. House sold, assets split… funny how losing what you thought was forever can feel like breathing again."

Sean insisted we celebrate Myles's freedom, my new security system, and Carlos's tech wizardry. We met at a buzzing downtown bistro, where Myles and Carlos dominated the conversation with outrageous college stories. Myles caught my eye every time Carlos embellished details, Myles's quiet laughter made my heart flutter.

I hadn't laughed that hard in years.

Later, as we stepped into the crisp night air, Myles walked me to my car.

"Thanks for tonight," he said, hands in his pockets.

"You needed it," I replied.

Then I saw it, a slip of paper tucked under my windshield wiper. Ice flooded my veins. I knew what it was before I even picked it up.

"What's that?" Myles frowned.

I snatched it with trembling fingers. The note was crisp, the handwriting meticulously neat:

Lani,
I'm going to make it right. I'll never stop loving you. I will show you.

No signature needed.

Myles took one look at my face and pulled out his phone. "We're filing another report. Now."

This time, I didn't hesitate. Because I finally understand, some people won't stop until you make them.

Chapter 21

Lani

I was at the police station again, sitting across from the detective. My fingers were laced together so tight my knuckles turned white. I walked him through every nightmarish detail: Darius's staged break-in, the hidden cameras, the note on my car. The officer listened carefully, his expression darkening, but when I finished, his response left me hollow.

"We can arrest him for violating the restraining order. Hopefully, the judge denies bail, or even better, he sets it so high he can't make bail." He said. "But beyond that, our hands are tied until he escalates further. "

My jaw clenched. "Escalates further? You mean until he hurts me?"

"I'm sorry, Ms. Shields." He sighed. "The law has limits. But keep reporting everything. If he contacts you again, call us immediately."

I left the station feeling powerless, but not broken.

Myles was leaning against his car, arms crossed, face unreadable. I loved that about him, how he let me take the lead, but stood ready as my shield. His presence alone was safety.

"What did they say?"

I shook my head. "They can arrest him for violating the restraining order, but that's it. Tthey can't guarantee they can hold him."

"Then we handle it ourselves." His voice was steel. "I'm staying at your place tonight. In case he's stupid enough to try something."

I opened my mouth to argue, then shut it. The truth? I didn't want to be alone.

We sat at my kitchen table, coffee going cold as we dissected every red flag I'd missed with Darius.

"At first, he was perfect," I admitted. "Charming. Attentive. Romantic. Nothing screamed '*danger.*'"

"They never do." Myles's grip tightened around his mug. "That's how guys like him operate. Hook you first, then show their teeth."

I rubbed my temples. "He talked about his memorabilia shop, how he opened it to honor his dad. It was his whole identity."

Myles's eyes sharpened. "That shop… it means everything to him?"

"According to him, his pride and joy," I confirmed.

A slow, dangerous smile curved his lips. "Good. Then we hit him there."

By morning, Myles had transformed my kitchen into a war room, laptop open, legal pads scrawled with notes.

"You can't control Darius," he said, "but you can make him regret crossing you, or at the very least think twice before doing it again. If he wants to terrorize you, we take what he loves most, his business."

I stared. "You think that'll work?"

"Only one way to find out."

He drafted a new lawsuit, so thorough it made my head spin: my new security system, apartment repairs, therapy costs, lost wages. And the final blow: pain and suffering.

"For compensation," Myles said, grinning, "we ask for his shop, or at least an amount so significant he can't pay without relinquishing it."

I barked a laugh. "You're so serious."

"I am, but also I'm efficient."

While he prepped the legal filings, I wrote Darius a letter, trying to be kind, but still firm. As a woman, I knew what it was like to witness aggression from men after rejection, so I wanted to avoid that at all costs. Clearly, the man did not have them all.

Darius,

I need you to understand that this isn't about hate, or revenge. I don't wish you any harm, but I do wish for peace in my life, peace I can't have if you continue down this path. The things you've done are not love, they're control, and manipulation. You do not love me, you might love the idea of me, but love can't exist where there's fear. You have created an environment of fear. Please, let me go. For both of our sake.

Respectfully,
Milani

I sealed it, unsure if he'd read it. But I needed to say it.

As the day wore on, I caught myself watching Myles, really watching him. The way his brow furrowed in concentration. The quiet confidence in his movements. The way he'd stepped into this mess without hesitation, not just offering comfort, but solutions.

He made me feel safe.

Without smothering me.

And that was the problem.

When he leaned against the counter, finishing his coffee, I realized with a jolt how my feelings had changed. I had let myself want to fall in love with this man. To let him be my rescuer. My person.

"Do you ever stop being a lawyer?" I teased, trying to lighten the mood.

He glanced up, smirking. "Do you ever stop being stubborn?"

We laughed, and for the first time in weeks, I felt light.

But this, him, was a risk I couldn't afford to take. Being a real friend meant not being selfish, even when your heart wants more. As vulnerable as I feel right now, I know he's on his own journey, and pushing for something more would be unfair to both of us. This might not be the right time and honestly, it might never be. And if I truly cared about him, I had to respect that, and be okay with it.

Chapter 22

Served. With another lawsuit. Like I was some monster. Like I hadn't loved her more than life itself.

This was Myles's doing. That smug bastard had poisoned her. Twisted her against me. Whispered in her ear until my Milani started believing his lies.

"You're not the man I thought you were."

She had no idea who I was. Who I had always been to her.

A love like we had was written in the stars for millennia. What I had sacrificed. What I had done, for us.

But love didn't end with paperwork. I didn't give up. And I didn't lose.

Especially not to him.

It started subtly. A black sedan parked just far enough behind my SUV to seem inconspicuous. At first, I chalked it up to coincidence. People parked on the street every day. But when it showed up in the lot near my office two days in a row, then again outside the gym, the unease started to creep in.

I told myself it was nothing. The stress of the situation with Lani, rebuilding trust, navigating her guardedness from her past with Michael, and now Darius. But it was hard to dismiss the pit in my stomach that twisted tighter with every glimpse of that same car in my rearview mirror.

Then, one afternoon, after a long lunch with Lani, I returned to my car to find it sitting unnaturally low. Confused, I crouched down and froze.

All four tires had been slashed.

Not punctured. Not flat from neglect, or a slow leak. Slashed, clean, surgical cuts. Deep enough to ruin the rubber entirely. My pulse kicked up as I stood, and scanned the street, heart thudding. Who would do something like this? A message? A warning? The questions were trivial, because I already knew the answer.

Darius.

He was pissed I beat his ass, and probably about the lawsuit, but none of that mattered.

I called Lani, keeping my voice calm, though my eyes never stopped scanning the area, half-expecting the vandal to still be lurking nearby. I didn't want to worry her unnecessarily, not with everything she'd already endured. Still, she was quiet on the other end of the phone, and I could tell her mind was racing from what I just told her.

"It's probably just some random vandal," she said finally. "Don't overthink it."

To keep her calm, I lied. "I know you're probably right, but just in case, be on the lookout when you are out and about."

But I didn't believe this was random. And neither did she.

The following week, I changed my routine. Different gym. Different parking spots. No social media check-ins. No predictable patterns.

It didn't help.

The black sedan showed up again outside my firm. Again near the corner store. It never followed directly. It never parked next to me. But it was always there somewhere.

Watching.

By the third time I saw the car, I started paying closer attention. I memorized the license plate, jotted it down, and even asked one of the firm's private investigators, casually, to see if it was linked to anything. The report came back clean. The vehicle was registered to a rental agency, leased out weeks ago to an out-of-town LLC with no clear owner.

Fed up with the back-and-forth, I headed straight for the car, ready to confront the driver after leaving my building that evening. The windows were tinted, making it impossible to see inside. My steps slowed as I reached the door and realized how foolish I must look. No one was inside. Worse yet, a rideshare light glowed in the window, mocking my paranoia.

Over the next few days things began to settle down, and I slipped back into some form of my daily routine. The sedan hadn't shadowed me in days. Maybe their routine changed. They got bored. switched vehicles, or they genuinely were not following me.

Then came that Thursday.

I left work late, the sky tinged orange with the fading sun. Exhausted, but eager to see Lani. We had plans for dinner at her place, something low-key. She'd been quieter than usual lately, and I had a feeling she was still carrying some tension about Darius. I didn't blame her. The guy was insane.

I turned onto Oakridge Avenue, the residential street that led to my place, and instantly, my stomach dropped.

Headlights in the rearview mirror. Too close. Then a revving engine.

My SUV jerked forward as the car behind me tapped the bumper. Once. Twice.

"What the…"

The third bump was harder.

I pressed the gas, veering slightly to the right to create distance. But the car behind me accelerated.

I reached for my phone, about to dial 911, when the high beams flashed, and suddenly, all I saw was white.

Blinded, I didn't see the sharp curve ahead. I didn't realize how fast I was going until I was already losing control.

The metal guardrail loomed in front of me like the edge of a cliff.

Because it was.

The crash was deafening.

Metal screamed. Glass shattered. Then silence.

I slumped against the airbag, chest heaving, dazed, but conscious. Every breath felt like a knife in my ribs. My vision swam. I reached for my phone, which had been thrown into the passenger footwell.

Then I heard it.

Footsteps.

Slow. Measured.

The back door of the SUV creaked open. A pause. I heard something fall, then the door clicked shut again.

I tried to lift my head, to see who it was, but all I caught was the faint scent of cologne, and the sound of shoes crunching gravel as the figure walked away.

Ten minutes, or what I could only imagine was ten minutes later, the world exploded again.

Not with tires, or impact, but with sirens.

Blue and red flooded the canyon walls, voices yelling, radios crackling.

I blinked hard as bright lights pierced the SUV's cabin. I moved slowly, trying to raise my hands up, to make myself visible.

But they didn't wait.

A voice boomed over a speaker. "Driver of the vehicle, exit the car with your hands above your head! Do not reach for anything!"

"I'm injured!" I shouted. "I can't!"

"Hands up! NOW!"

I tried. God, I tried.

But the moment my hand reached for the seat belt buckle, everything turned to chaos.

Gunshots rang out. The glass exploded again.

And I crumpled in pain.

Chapter 24

I sat in a silent apartment, in the glow of my laptop. Live scanner reports confirmed it: police activity in Blue Lake Canyon. One male shot. Believed armed and dangerous. The call originated from an "anonymous tip" about a "black male in his late 30s in a late-model white SUV headed east on Oakridge brandishing a gun and making threats towards a woman. The suspect is down, requesting medical assistance."

I smiled.

I didn't want to kill Myles. Not yet. That would be too fast. Too final.

But removing him?

Making him want to remove himself?

Now that was just the beginning.

Chapter 25

The hospital walls felt too white, too clean, like they were trying to mask the mess within them. I sat in a stiff vinyl chair outside Room 307, legs crossed tightly, arms wrapped around myself like I could fold into nothingness.

When the call came through, I thought it had to be a mistake. "You're listed as Mr. Myles Parker's emergency contact."

What?

My phone nearly slipped from my hand. I had gone out of my way to draw boundaries. How the hell was I his first point of contact? I didn't even remember ever filling anything out. My first instinct was to correct them, hang up, and protect my peace.

Then they said it.

"He's been shot."

Everything blurred after that.

Now here I was, breathing antiseptic air, and counting every second in my head. Two uniformed police officers stood guard nearby. I'd never known anyone who'd been shot before, so I guessed this was standard protocol.

Every time someone in scrubs passed, I shot to my feet, only to be met with a tired, "Soon," or "We're still stabilizing him."

The emergency contact thing? I filed it away. I'd ask him later, if he made it back to me.

Eventually, a doctor approached, kind eyes, weary shoulders.

"Ms. Shields? He's stable. The bullets missed all major organs, but there was significant blood loss. He's lucky to be alive."

I nodded, swallowing hard. "Can I see him?"

"Not yet. He's still under investigation. The detectives in charge will need to authorize your visitation."

"Investigation?" I repeated, dazed. I sank back into my seat.

Two hours later, a detective arrived, stone-faced, and professional. He extended a hand.

"Good evening. I'm Detective Imere. I'm leading this investigation."

I shook his hand, still in shock.

"Can you tell me what's going on?" I asked, my voice thin. "Was this Darius?"

The detective paused. "Would that be Darius McRay?"

"Oh my God. Please tell me he didn't shoot Myles. This is all my fault."

Tears spilled out, fast and unrelenting.

The detective tried to reassure me gently. "Mr. Parker wasn't shot by Mr. McRay. However, we have reason to believe he was the target of a swatting incident."

"Swatting?" I repeated, blinking.

"An anonymous caller reported a man matching Mr. Parker's description brandishing a weapon and threatening a woman. No victim was found. No witnesses other than the anonymous caller. Just a false report meant to provoke a tactical response. Before you mentioned McRay, I was going to ask if you knew anyone who might want to harm Mr. Parker. Let's step inside. I'd like to update him and see if he can fill in some gaps."

I followed him into the cold, sterile room. Myles lay there, motionless, ashen, handcuffed to the bed. The detective stepped back out into the hallway to ask one of the uniformed officers to remove the cuffs.

"How are you feeling, Mr. Parker?" Detective Imere asked when he returned.

Myles groaned. "I have definitely been better, getting shot hurts like hell."

"We found black paint transfer on your vehicle, consistent with a 2022 Lexus ES. Does that mean anything to you?"

Myles squinted. "I remember leaving work, heading home before meeting Lani. I heard a car rev its engine and accelerate. Saw it tap my bumper. Then blinding lights, maybe blinders? They rammed me. I crashed." Myles's memories were coming in pieces.

"That tracks," Imere replied.

"What do you mean?"

"Tire marks suggest a deliberate push. The guardrail almost gave way. If a tree hadn't caught your back end, you might not be here."

Myles exhaled sharply.

"Anything else come to mind?"

"Yeah. I've seen a black sedan tailing me. Weeks now. Had an investigator from my firm run the plates, rental agency."

My stomach flipped. That same car had been parked near my place. I'd ignored it.

"Can I get the investigator's name?"

"Artis Renard. And... after I crashed, I think I heard a door. Footsteps. But it's fuzzy. Then lights, and cops shouting." Myles scratched his head, obviously annoyed with his recollection of events.

"That makes sense," Detective Imere said. "We found a gun in your car. No prints. It was stolen years ago, linked to a stalking case in Detroit."

I felt the blood drain from my face.

"The lead suspect in that case?" Detective Imere continued. "Darius McRay, at least that is what he was going by at the time. It seems to have been an alias."

We both gasped.

"I'm in touch with the detective from that case. We'll coordinate and take it from there. Here's my card."

He handed one to each of us and left.

The silence afterward was deafening. The only sound was the soft beeping of machines.

I stood by Myles's bedside emotions from this evening crashing into me. Then Myles smiled weakly.

"Hey, Trouble."

"You scared the hell out of me."

"I tend to do that to women," he joked, then winced. "Hurts to be charming."

I laughed, softly, and sat by his side. His hand curled around mine as he drifted off to sleep.

I didn't move.

This man had every reason to push me away, but he didn't. He didn't blame me for bringing any of this craziness into his life; he just constantly showed up and showed out for me.

Maybe he was the one I should've chosen all along. We had a rough start, but even with that, I could tell Myles was not a bad person.

The thought stirred hope in me.

The quiet of home had never felt so comforting. No hospital machines beeping, no sterile air, no harsh lights. Just the familiar rhythm of life, Lani's soft footsteps, the clink of mugs in the sink, and her humming in the kitchen. Since I got discharged, she hadn't left my side.

She hovered like a hawk, fluffing pillows, reheating soup, fussing if I so much as lifted my arm too fast. She'd taken over my couch, curled up in a blanket, giving me the kind of care I didn't know I needed.

"You know, I think you might've missed your calling as a live-in nurse," I teased one afternoon, smirking at the TV.

"Don't tempt me," she fired back, tossing a grape at me. "I've got schedules, alarms, and notes. This is a professional setup." It was very domestic. Almost like a peek into our ideal future, well without the getting shot part. I loved every second of it.

Every morning, I woke to the scent of fresh coffee, and her voice humming over the soft clatter of dishes. Every night, she made sure I didn't forget a single dose of medication, even when I said I was fine. She slid into the space beside me like she belonged there.

But I could feel it, her guilt. It hung around her like a second shadow. I wasn't angry about that. I understood it.

Still, I didn't want her carrying that weight.

Out of the blue, while reruns of The Wire murmured in the background, and sunset painted the walls amber, she turned to me with a look I couldn't quite read. "Myles," she said softly, "can I ask you something?"

"Shoot," I answered. She gave me a look. "Bad joke. I get it."

"When did you list me as your emergency contact?"

That caught me off guard. "That's what's been on your mind?"

"Yes," she said. "I never filled anything out, but when they called me... I was the one they reached. Not your parents. Or your ex-wife. Me? I almost hung up on those people,"she chuckled, easing some of the seriousness in the moment.

I rubbed the back of my neck. "A couple of months ago."

Her eyes narrowed."Why?"

I didn't look away. "Because I trust you." She didn't say anything, so I went on. "You're the only person I've really let in, Lani. My family's not here, and if anything ever happened... I'd want it to be you who made decisions for me. You've always been honest with me, even when it was hard. You didn't take advantage. You kept your boundaries, and respected mine. That means more than I can explain."

She blinked at me like she didn't know how to respond. That wall she keeps up, the one built from years of pain, was cracking. And in that silence, I felt it. If I had asked her for more than friendship right then, she would've said yes. But I didn't. I wanted her to choose that when she was ready. Not because of guilt or fear, but because she wanted to be with me.

After that, things settled into a new normal. Coffee in the mornings. Slow walks in the afternoons. She read me random trivia while I rested. Her things made their way into every room, a cardigan here, a hair tie there. Her scent from her body butter lingered on everything, including me.

I heard her rummaging through the bathroom shelf, then silence. That kind of silence that meant I was about to get caught up.

"Now I know I didn't use this much," Lani muttered, mostly to herself, but loud enough for me to hear.

I winced, adjusting my shirt as I walked past the mirror. I knew exactly what she'd found.

"Myles!" she called. "Have you been using my body butter?"

I stepped into the doorway with a sheepish grin. "Depends... Is it the one that smells like cake? Does it make your skin feel like velvet?"

She spun around with her arms crossed, and that eyebrow raised, the one that made her look both beautiful and mildly dangerous. "So that's a yes?"

I shrugged, and pointed to my shoulder where a few faint scratches were healing. "I've been using it on these. You know shea butter helps with the scarring. Stuff works wonders."

She squinted at me, lips twitching like she was trying not to laugh. "So you don't mind walking around smelling like *Amber and Vanilla*?"

I chuckled. "Absolutely not. I smell like a damn snack. Ask anybody."

That got her. She laughed, this rich, soft sound that always settled something in me. But then it shifted, just for a second. Her eyes locked with mine, and the moment stretched a little longer than it should have. The kind of look that made my chest tighten and my brain short circuit.

She broke eye contact first, grabbing the jar and moving toward the door. She looked down. "You had the audacity to use my expensive body butter and didn't even bother to moisturize those ashy ankles!? Well, go ahead and add this to your Amazon cart, Mr. Snack. You're going to need your own. You're not going to keep stealing mine."

The next morning, I groaned dramatically trying to sit up, just to hear her scoff. "You winced like you climbed Everest," she said. "All you did was stand."

"It's part of the recovery," I joked.

"From where I'm standing, it looks like someone's milking his injuries for pancakes."

I grinned. "Guilty. What gave me away?"

"The pancake mix was already out. Again."

"I appreciate the care," I said with mock innocence.

"You're such a con artist."

"But I'm your favorite one," I winked. She rolled her eyes and turned to walk away, but I stopped her.

"Lani?" She glanced over her shoulder. "Will you go on a date with me?" She froze. "I mean, a real one. Not because of pity or guilt. And not lunch either. Just… a real date. I feel like I am ready, and hopefully you are too."

"Yes," she said before I could finish.

"Yeah?" I was low-key shocked she agreed.

"Yeah. As long as you don't fake a limp."

"No promises. But I'll bring flowers."

She turned back to the kitchen, and I leaned back, grinning like an idiot. Because for once, something felt like it was finally going right.

Chapter 27

I curled up on the couch with a glass of red wine in hand, while Sean stretched out at the other end. The soft, velvety voice of Anita Baker drifted through the speakers, the perfect backdrop for a much-needed girls' night. I had successfully nursed Myles back to health and was back in my apartment.

"So," Sean began, taking a sip of her wine, "what's the latest with Darius? You haven't mentioned him in a minute. Is the investigation still going on? It's still hard to believe he did all that to poor Myles."

I nodded and let out a long sigh. "Yeah. As far as I can prove, it's been quiet. They tried to bring him in for questioning, but he vanished. I don't know if I'm being paranoid, but anytime I see a car tailing me too close or I feel eyes on me in public, the hairs on my arms raise on end and goosebumps race over my skin.

The detectives say he cleaned out the townhouse. Get this, the memorabilia shop he claimed was the biggest part of him, the one his dad supposedly left him, never existed. The building he claimed to be occupying hadn't been leased in two years. They don't know how deep this all goes, but he's definitely a fraud.

None of that makes me feel any better, knowing I let someone like that get close to me, into my space. Even with the new security system and locks, I don't have peace of mind. I'm still on edge, still looking over my shoulder. Turns out nothing was actually registered in his name. It was all buried under different LLCs and shell companies. They don't even know this man's real name at this point. It's like he's a ghost. He can be anywhere watching, lurking in the shadows, which makes this situation more terrifying. I have no idea where he went, but honestly? As long as he stays away from me and mine, I'll be okay. Although, with my luck, I know the chances of that happening are slim to none."

Sean studied my face with a long, thoughtful look. "And you're sure you're okay? Because if I need to stay on high alert, you know I will."

I smiled. "I promise I'm good. For the first time in a long time, I feel like I can breathe, even if it's just a little."

Sean grinned. "That's what I like to hear. Now, let's talk about something more interesting. Like you and Myles."

I laughed, shaking my head. "What about me and Myles?"

"Oh, don't play coy. You've been dropping his name into conversation a lot lately," she teased. "He's been your knight in shining armor through all of this. You can't tell me you haven't thought about letting that man out of the friend zone."

I sighed, my cheeks warming. "Fine. I've thought about it. He's been amazing, calm, supportive, always stepping up. And most of all, he didn't blame me for any of what happened. Even though, I think we both know it was kind of my fault. But the man just got divorced, I'm not trying to be anybody's rebound."

Sean raised an eyebrow. "True. But people don't always rebound. Sometimes they just realize what they want. Maybe he's one of those people. You'll figure it out. Just don't overthink yourself out of something good."

I nodded slowly, but before I could respond, Sean's face lit up.

"Speaking of good things… guess who thinks Carlos is about to pop the question?"

"Wait, what?" I sat up, forgetting about my wine.

"We've been talking about marriage," she said, smiling, "and last week, he slipped and said, *when we're married*… I think he's planning something."

"Do you think it's too soon?" I asked, torn between awe and caution.

"Nope," she replied without hesitation. "When you know, you know. I know Carlos is it for me."

I grinned. "Well, I better be your maid of honor."

"Obviously."

The night flowed with laughter and R&B love songs. We sang at the top of our lungs, completely off key. The wine made us forget neither of us had any type of musical ability. For the first time in a while, I felt hopeful.

The next morning, I opened my laptop and blinked at the notification on screen: a massive custom order, the largest I'd ever received. My heart raced as I read the details: a full spread of my baked goods requested by Saunders & Wright, a prestigious law firm in Stonebrook.

"Wow," I whispered. "This is huge."

Excited, I decided to bring my followers along for the journey. I went live on social media, walking them through inventory checks, shopping, and kitchen prep.

The comments rolled in, excited, encouraging, filled with hearts, and fire emojis.

But one username, jd_86, stood out. Their comments were not celebratory; they seemed really personal. Oddly familiar, and full of questions.

It threw me off, but I finished the stream and saved the chat log for Detective Imere. It could be nothing. Or it could be Darius. Either way, better safe than sorry.

The morning of the delivery was hectic, but everything came together. My car was packed with neatly packaged tarts, cookies, and mini cakes. Arriving at the sleek high-rise of Saunders & Wright, I took a deep breath.

As I stepped through the office doors, the first person I saw was Myles, holding a carton of milk.

"Myles?" I blurted, surprised.

He turned and grinned, dimples on full display. "Good morning, Milani."

"You work here?"

"Guilty," he said. "I had a feeling you'd be stopping by today."

Realization hit me. "You set this up, didn't you?"

He shrugged, a twinkle in his eye. "I may have suggested to my colleagues that your baked goods were the best in town. And I wasn't lying."

As I unpacked the treats, Myles hovered nearby, chatting like normal.

"Let's see if your tarts are as good as I remember," he said, picking one up.

One bite, and he groaned in delight. "Lani… this is incredible. The flaky crust, the fruit is the perfect amount of sweet and tart. I feel like there is a party on my tongue."

I laughed, a nervous laugh because of how he savored the tart. Watching him thoroughly enjoy and savor something I created had me hot and bothered. He was definitely speaking my love language, and I don't even think he was aware.

His gaze locked with mine. "You're amazing, you know that? Talented, smart, beautiful… I was an idiot to mess up the first time. But now that I'm fully free, and you've agreed to go on a real date with me, what do you say? Friday night at eight?"

I hesitated. Sean's voice echoed in my head about rebounds.

Myles caught it, and smiled. "Think about it. No rush. But I'll be calling you," he said with a wink before walking off to his meeting.

Chapter 28

The following week, I was browsing the stalls at the local farmer's market when my phone buzzed. I glanced at the screen and saw Myles's name. Instantly, butterflies flitted in my stomach as I answered.

"Hello?" I said, trying to keep my voice casual.

"Hey, Lani," Myles's smooth, rich voice greeted me. I couldn't help the big, goofy grin that spread across my face.

"Hey, Myles. What's up?"

We exchanged a bit of small talk, my recent baking adventures, and his work at the firm. Then Myles shifted gears. "So, I was thinking... how about we do dinner? Not coffee or lunch like before, dinner. Me being a gentleman picking you up from your door in my car. The whole nine yards with maybe a good night kiss for good measure. What do you say?"

Dinner.

My heart skipped a beat. This wasn't our usual friendly lunch dates. This was intentional. This man is intentionally trying to date me.

"I'd like that," I said, trying to sound nonchalant despite the excitement bubbling inside me.

"Great. Friday night, I'll pick you up at eight."

When Myles arrived Friday evening, his sleek black Audi RS 7 gleamed in the parking lot, freshly detailed. He stepped out, dressed in a sharp blazer over a fitted black turtleneck and dark jeans. I took a moment to appreciate the man in front of me.

He opened my car door, waiting for me to step in. "Beautiful car," I commented as I slid into the seat, the leather cool against my legs.

He smiled, closing the door behind me. As he got in, he looked over and said, "The car's nice, but it looks a hell of a lot better with you in it."

My inner voice screamed, *Okayyyyyy girl!*

Instead of heading to a fancy, reservations-only restaurant like I expected, Myles asked me, "What's your favorite food?"

"Tandoori chicken," I replied without hesitation.

With a nod, he drove across town to a tiny hole-in-the-wall Indian restaurant tucked between a laundromat and a discount store. I was surprised at first, but when we stepped inside, the aromas of spices and freshly baked naan wrapped around me like a warm hug.

The restaurant wasn't much to look at. Worn furniture, faded walls, but the staff made up for it with their welcoming smiles and attentive service. It was clear Myles was a regular. The banter between him and the servers was playful and familiar.

When the food arrived, I was blown away. The tandoori chicken was perfectly charred and flavorful, the samosas crisp and savory, and the mango lassi was perfect, creamy, and sweet.

"You forgot I'm a foodie, didn't you?" Myles teased, watching me devour my plate.

I laughed, wiping my mouth with a napkin. "I did, but I'll never doubt you again. You know all the hidden gems."

Stuffed and satisfied, we wrapped up the remaining dinner, but I could tell Myles wasn't quite ready for the night to end.

"Feel like taking a walk by the docks?" he asked as we got back in the car.

I hesitated. "I'd love to, but these booties are hella cute, and unfortunately they aren't exactly made for walking."

Without a word, Myles pulled into the mall parking lot.

"What are we doing here?" I asked, confused.

He parked and turned to me. "What size shoe do you wear?"

"Uh… eight and a half. Why?"

"Be right back."

Before I could argue, Myles jumped out of the car and disappeared into the mall. I sat there, stunned. Pulling out my phone, I called Sean.

"Girl," I said as soon as she answered. "You won't believe this man right now!"

"What did he do?" Sean asked, already laughing.

"He just ran into the mall to buy me shoes so we can walk along the docks. Shoes, Sean. What kind of man does this? How thoughtful is that?"

"A problem solver. The kind who wants to show you he's here for a long time, not just a good time," Sean said.

I was still reeling when Myles returned ten minutes later, a Nordstrom bag in hand. He handed it to me, and inside was a pair of Hokas and socks, in a colorway that just so happened to match my outfit.

I stared at the shoes, then at Myles in shock.

"I pay attention," he said simply, a small smile on his face. "Whatever I have to do, however long it takes, I'm here for it."

My inner self practically screamed, *YASSSSSSS BITCHHHHHH!*

I slid the ankle socks and Hokas on, feeling like Cinderella in glass slippers, except these were far more practical. As we walked along the docks under the moonlight, hand in hand, I couldn't help but think that maybe, just maybe, Myles was worth breaking my own rules for.

Not to mention, if he kept this up, I would definitely need to take Sean and Carlos out for an apology/thank you brunch.

Chapter 29

Myles was setting an impossibly high bar. Each date he planned was more thoughtful, more personal, like he was trying to prove that he really saw me, knew me, and valued me. And maybe he was.

Tonight was no different.

I had just wrapped up my live stream when a knock came at the door, interrupting my post-baking cleanup. Instinctively, I checked the cameras, a habit I picked up after everything that happened with Darius. Seeing Myles on the screen, looking casually fine in a pale blue linen button-down shirt which he wore partially unbuttoned, and white linen pants, I smiled and opened the door.

"Pack a bag," he said, all cool and nonchalant. But that grin? Mischievous as hell.

"We're going to the beach."

Ten minutes later, we were on the road in his sleek convertible. The top was down, the breeze playing in my curls while the sun dipped low behind the horizon, painting the sky in streaks of red, orange, and purple. The night air wrapped around us like a soft blanket.

When we pulled up to the beach, my jaw dropped. Right there in the sand was a full-blown luxury picnic, like something off of a Pinterest board. I can only imagine he went to the designer and asked for an Arabian Nights theme. Everything was jewel-toned, with rich magenta, teal, gold, and deep purples. In the center sat an extravagantly decorated table that sat low to the ground, surrounded by glowing lanterns, candles, and more pillows than we could ever need.

It took my breath away.

He had even brought my favorite foods: tandoori chicken and garlic naan from that tiny Indian place we went to on our first date, cheesecake from the farmer's market, and a deck of Uno cards. Smooth R&B floated from a nearby speaker. Every single detail screamed I thought this through.

"Myles," I whispered. "This is... breathtaking."

He smiled at me with those warm eyes. "You're breathtaking."

"Seriously, how did you know to do all of this?" "

"I listen, Lani. Everything you say is important to me. I'm very thankful you choose to share yourself with me, so every opportunity I get I am going to celebrate you in a way that you know is just for you."

"Are you trying to get brownie points, Myles?"

"Absolutely." He smirked.

The night was pure magic.

The moonlight, the candlelight, the way I kept beating him in Uno, and he kept pretending to be surprised. We laughed, so hard my cheeks hurt. I couldn't remember the last time I'd felt so light, so free.

The wind had calmed some by the time we settled deeper into the pillows on the beach. The candles flickered gently around us, casting warm halos over the food, and flickering in Myles's eyes whenever he looked my way. It could've been a scene pulled straight from a dream: gorgeous setup, amazing food, the right music, and the right man. But even as I laughed through another round of Uno, something in my chest stayed tight.

"Alright," Myles said, drawing a card from the pile. "I'm convinced you're cheating."

I feigned innocence, raising an eyebrow. "Excuse me?"

He pointed at the cards in my hand. "You're cheating! You put a draw two on top of a draw four!"

"Says who?"

"Says every official Uno rule in the universe," he said, dramatically gasping.

"Well, that's how we played in my house. When in Rome, sir!"I laughed, tucking the rogue card back into my hand. "I'm going to give it to you this time. But next time, we're playing house rules, and your ass is grass."

"I am weak," he said, throwing his head back.

It felt good to laugh like that, to pretend for just a moment that the only thing that mattered was who won the next hand.

But when I looked down at my cards again, my smile faded a little. I couldn't help but revisit my past decisions, and how they had impacted my life. Especially in moments when I wanted so badly to let another person close to me. My smile slipped, but I quickly put it back into place, and I held onto it anyway. I had to. Still, Myles must've seen my expression shift, because he set his cards down and leaned closer.

"What's going on?" he asked softly.

I hesitated, then sighed. "I don't know. I guess, it's hard to let myself just enjoy this."

He didn't say anything, just waited, which made it easier to keep going.

"I keep thinking about Darius. About how I didn't see it coming. How I let someone that dangerous so close. After Michael, I swore I'd be smarter. More careful. And I thought I was." I shook my head, voice tightening. "But look where that got me. Again."

Myles's hand found mine. He didn't try to stop me. He didn't give some cliché speech about how it wasn't my fault. H e j u s t listened.

I took a shaky breath. "Sometimes I feel like I don't know how to trust my own judgment anymore."

He squeezed my hand gently. "Then let me help you carry it."

I looked up, caught in the seriousness of his tone.

"I mean it, Lani. I'm not here just to have a few nice dates and disappear. I see you. I value you. And I know what you've been through. That doesn't scare me. If anything, it makes me respect you even more, it makes me want to be more careful with you and your heart because I know you've been with men who were careless."

I blinked back unexpected tears.

He smiled then, a soft, crooked thing. "Also, I'm too emotionally invested now. I've let you beat me in Uno."

I laughed wetly, dabbing under my eyes. "You're ridiculous."

"Guilty." He replied.

Later, we walked along the shoreline, our feet sinking into the cool sand with every step. The waves whispered against the shore, a gentle soundtrack to our quiet.

"Lani," he said, stopping beneath the moonlight.

I turned to face him, my heart thudding.

And then... he kissed me. It was completely unexpected, but definitely wanted.

It wasn't rushed. It wasn't uncertain. It was soft, warm, full of promise. And suddenly, nothing else mattered. I didn't know how much I yearned for that intimacy until our lips touched, and his tongue parted mine. I tried to pour every ounce of passion left in my body into that kiss. My hands went searching for an anchor point, finding his neck trying to pull him in more. His hands found my waist, and attempted to pull me even closer. Any closer we would have been in each other's skin. When we finally pulled away from each other, we were both breathless.

"I never thought this was in the cards for me," Myles said, his voice low. "After failing at marriage... then meeting the perfect woman, and getting stuck in the friend zone." He gave me a half smile. "I'm glad you finally gave me a shot. Like I said on our first date, however long it takes."

He kissed me again, deeper this time.

By the time he walked me to my door, I felt like I was floating. That night had been everything. Thoughtful. Romantic. Perfect.

I hummed to myself while getting ready for bed, still tasting his kiss, still glowing.

Then my phone buzzed.

I reached for it, expecting a sweet goodnight from Myles.

But it wasn't him.

It was an unsaved number.

One word.

Unknown: Why?

Just that. One question. Cold. Sharp.

My heart dropped.

And just like that, the warmth of the night instantly dissipated.

The next morning, Myles and I sat across from Detective Imere at a quiet table in a secure office at the precinct. I clutched a folder in my lap, stuffed with printouts, screenshots, and notes I'd been collecting over the last few weeks. Myles sat close beside me, his fingers brushing mine under the table, a quiet, steady reassurance.

Detective Imere placed a manila file on the table and let out a slow breath. "I got in touch with the lead investigator on the Detroit case. It paints a pretty grim picture."

I leaned in, my stomach already knotting. "What did they find?"

"Darius has a history there. He stalked a young woman he'd gone to college with, someone he reconnected with online years later. She was already in a relationship at the time. At first, it seemed like he just had a thing for her. Then things escalated fast."

He opened the file and turned it toward us. I glanced down at the photos and documents. "He shot her boyfriend. Left him paralyzed, and in a vegetative state. She disappeared shortly after the incident, and so did Darius. The DA never moved forward with prosecution because the witness and McRay both vanished. No additional witnesses, no cooperative parties."

My stomach turned. I blinked hard, trying to hold myself together. "He's done this before," I whispered.

Imere nodded, his face grim. "Same pattern. Quiet obsession, escalation. Then he disappears when it all blows up or he can't find his victim."

Swallowing against the dryness in my throat, I dug into my purse to pull out my phone. "I... I got a message last night. I don't know if it helps, but maybe it can be traced."

I showed him the screen. One message. One word: *Why?*

He studied the screen. "We'll send this to the tech unit. I can't make any promises, though. If he's smart, which I'm sure he is since he has managed to evade Detroit PD for two years, I am almost certain he's using a burner. It will probably be untraceable."

"There's something else," I say. "During a live stream a couple of weeks ago, there was this user asking overly personal questions. It felt off. Like they knew me too well or were trying to get a reaction. I ignored it and kept going, but I made a note of it just in case."

Myles shifts beside me. "Wait... was the screen name 'jd_86'?"

I turn to him slowly. "Yes. Why?"

He rubbed the back of his neck and grinned sheepishly. "That was... me."

"What?"

"I knew you had that big order coming up, and I wanted to be spontaneous, drop a few subtle hints: JD_86, Juris Doctor, and my birth year. I thought it was romantic. You were so busy, I figured it'd be cute to pop up anonymously. Like a secret admirer."

"Myles! I have a whole-ass stalker who is responsible for you getting shot! What do you mean you thought it would be romantic?" I couldn't keep my laughter in.

"My bad, I guess I might have been doing too much." He grinned sheepishly.

I folded my arms with a smirk. "If circumstances were different, I could see it. Too bad it came off creepy. Try again next time, smooth operator."

Detective Imere raised an eyebrow but chuckled along with us. Due to what we were just discussing, we collectively needed that laugh.

He handed the phone off to a tech officer who entered the room. "We'll run it through our systems and see if anything pings. But like I said, don't hold your breath. If he's covering his tracks, we're going to need a slip-up."

I nodded, feeling a little steadier. "I just want this to be over. For good."

"And we will get him," Imere said firmly. "We're closer now than we've ever been."

As we left the station, I slipped my hand into Myles's for some much-needed comfort. The weight wasn't completely lifted, but something inside me felt just a little bit lighter.

Chapter 31

Months had passed since the chaos, and with every day, Myles and I had grown more comfortable, more in sync. What had once been cautious conversations and gentle flirtations had blossomed into a rhythm that felt effortless. We cherished each other and never missed a chance to show it.

Tonight, popcorn popped in the background while Myles set out two beers on the coffee table. I curled up in my usual corner of the couch, a thick blanket wrapped around my legs, and my hair pulled into a puff on top of my head. No makeup, just a bare face, and according to my baby, still beautiful.

"All right," Myles said, sliding in next to me and picking up the remote. "You ready for this?"

"What are we watching?" I asked.

"One guess." He cleared his throat and launched into a flawless impersonation. "Well, damn, did you at least pinch the bitch?"

"Players Club," I laughed. "Good choice, grasshopper. Good choice indeed!"

"One of these days, I'm going to trip you up and finally be king of this movie thing," he said, grabbing me and tickling until I squealed in surrender.

"Keep trying, mister king," I managed between giggles.

I nudged him with my foot. "Don't tickle me again, or I'll bring out the big boys." I made little pinching claws with my fingers.

He laughed and let me mock-chase him around the couch for a few minutes before we collapsed back onto the cushions.

As the opening credits rolled, we tossed out movie quotes like tennis volleys, laughing, challenging, and teasing each other. These nights, quiet, cozy, full of banter, had become our favorite ritual.

But tonight wasn't just about movies.

It was the night before Sean and Carlos's wedding, the first major event we would attend as a couple.

"You ready to be on display tomorrow?" Myles asked, his voice softer now.

"As ready as I'll ever be," I said, resting my head on his shoulder. "We've been soft-launching for months. Might as well make it official."

"You nervous?"

"Not really. You?"

He grinned. "I'm looking forward to hearing your speech."

"Oh, I'm definitely taking it back," I said confidently. "I've known Sean since kindergarten. I've got stories in the vault. But I'll keep it short and sweet. I got this."

The day of the wedding, we stood in the golden light of early evening as it filtered through the garden canopy, bathing everything in a warm, honeyed glow. Rows of white chairs were lined with lavender sprigs and silver eucalyptus, but none of that held a candle to what I saw next.

Sean stepped into view, and I swear the whole world stopped spinning for just a second.

She looked like she had stepped out of a dream, her gown hugging her curves like it was sewn by angels, glittering beading catching every last bit of sun, and her skin glowing like she'd swallowed starlight. Her hair was up in a soft, sculptural bun, curls pinned delicately with crystal combs. And her face? Flawless. Not because of the makeup, but because she was happy.

"Well, who knew?" Myles muttered beside me. "The girl cleans up good."

"Don't play with me, my bestie has always been THAT GIRL." I whispered, never taking my eyes off her.

Carlos was waiting under the arch, clearly trying not to cry. He looked incredible in his ivory tux and black lapels, but it was his face that made me melt, completely in awe of the woman walking toward him.

The ceremony began, the officiant welcoming everyone with that gentle, calming voice. "We are here to celebrate the union of two souls who knew from the start they were meant for each other," she said.

Honestly? Truer words hadn't been spoken.

When it was time for the vows, Carlos went first. He took Sean's hands and looked at her like the rest of us had disappeared.

"Sean," he said, voice steady, "from the moment I met you, I knew my life was about to change. You are the calm to my chaos, the rhythm to my heart, the laughter I never knew I needed. You challenge me, inspire me, and love me with a depth I didn't think I deserved."

He took a breath, eyes never leaving hers. "Today, I vow to protect your joy, uplift your dreams, and honor your heart. I vow to never stop learning you, even when I think I know you completely. I vow to be your partner in the mundane and the magical. And above all, I vow to choose you, every day, in every lifetime."

I was already in tears, but when Sean spoke, it was game over.

"Carlos," she began, and her voice cracked just slightly, "loving you feels like breathing, natural, essential, undeniable. From our first conversation, I felt seen. You never tried to tame my fire; you danced in it with me."

She laughed a little, then continued. "You've held space for every version of me: the dreamer, the doubter, the warrior, the woman. I promise to pour into you the way you've poured into me. To build a home of peace, passion, and Sunday morning pancakes. I promise to walk beside you, not ahead, not behind, but hand in hand, always. I choose you. Forever."

I couldn't even pretend to hold it together. It was one of the most beautiful things I had ever witnessed.

After the officiant pronounced them husband and wife, Carlos kissed her like we had all disappeared, like nothing existed outside of that moment except him, her, and the love they shared. The crowd cheered, and Myles wrapped an arm around me.

"Now that's a love story," I said softly.

He nodded. "Ours is next."

And for the first time in a long time, I believed it with my whole heart.

The reception was intimate, lively, and filled with love.

When it was Myles's turn to toast, he stood and tapped his glass. "This isn't just a wedding. It's a celebration of two people who are exactly where they're supposed to be," he said. "Congratulations, out of all the people in the world, you found each other. That's a beautiful thing."

Then he turned toward me. "You both gave me a glimpse of what real partnership looks like. And because of that... I found my own piece of happiness too."

Tears shimmered in my eyes as the room clinked glasses and cheered.

Then it was my turn.

I stepped up with my phone and a mischievous grin "Sean and I go way back. Like hair bows and beads back. Ashy knees and missing teeth back."

Laughter rippled through the room.

"She wasn't always sweet. Our first day of kindergarten, I had my little eight-pack of crayons. Sean rolled up with a 64-pack with the sharpener. I asked to color with her. She said, 'No'. I wasn't used to that word, so I reached anyway."

More laughter.

"She snatched those crayons so fast, I thought Barry Allen had entered the room. After making me wait what felt like ages, she finally said, 'You can color with me only if you promise to always be my friend.'"

I looked at Sean. "And here we are. Still together. Still coloring life side by side. We have had a few new characters to join us on the journey, but we are still at it. I love you, best friend. As for Carlos you aight, as long as you keep that smile on my bestie's face. But seriously blessings on your union, thanks for providing all of us with a visual of what it looks like to love, and to be loved out loud."

Sniffles, and applause followed.

I sat, then popped back up. "Oh! After the honeymoon, see me. I owe y'all a thank-you brunch."

I winked at Myles, and raised my glass.

Later, on the rooftop of our hotel, city lights twinkled below us. Myles laid out a blanket.

"You didn't tell me there was a rooftop," I said.

"Had to save something for the end," he replied. "Come here."

We lay back, watching the stars.

"What do you think our future looks like?" I asked.

"Like this," he said. "More movies. More surprises. Eventually, some little bad-ass kids running around our forever home."

"You're serious?" I asked.

"I've never been more sure."

I took his hand. "Just don't ever stop making me laugh."

"Deal. As long as you don't stop doing that little thing I like."

I smacked his arm, laughing. "You so nasty!"

We laughed, and the moment stretched sweet and slow, an ending that felt like a perfect beginning.

Chapter 32

The motel reeked of bleach and stale cigarette smoke. The kind of place no one asked questions. Where people disappeared without consequence. Some by choice. Most not.

I sat on the edge of the lumpy mattress, the crusty comforter scrunched beneath me ironically providing no comfort. The buzzing fluorescent above the bathroom sink flickered in a broken rhythm, like it was counting down to something. Something I knew was coming. Something I didn't want to face yet.

I hadn't really slept in days. Not truly. Every creak outside my door, every car that lingered too long in the lot, had me reaching for the burner under my pillow. I'd learned to survive with disposable phones as my only connection to the outside world, swapping them every couple of days. Yesterday, I compromised one after staying too long on one of her lives. I smashed it under my boot, then dumped the SIM behind a gas station to cover my tracks.

The news had gone quiet. Too damn quiet. That's what kept me on edge.

I swiped open the screen again. Her stream had ended hours ago, but I sat here staring at the screenshot. In her eyes, I see our future, just the two of us loving each other, fully devoted to one another. In reality, Lani sits in her little pastel kitchen, piping icing on cupcakes like the world hadn't tilted off its axis. Laughing. Smiling. Living. Probably playing house with that soft-ass clown, Myles.

That's what pissed me off the most.

Myles. That smug, pretty boy punk.

He should've known better. Should've read the signs and backed the hell off. But no, Myles had to be the hero. He took the SWAT hit and somehow still came out on top. He walked away with my girl like he earned her.

I stared at the frozen frame of her mid-laugh, caressing the phone softly, envisioning my hands on her skin. I zoomed in until I could see the damn flour dusted on her cheek. My breath fogged the screen. She looked happy.

"She still thinks you're the safe choice or the best choice, but I will show her," I whispered, low and sinister.

Then quieter, more to myself, "She thinks this is over."

I leaned forward, elbows to knees, fists clenched tight. The spirals were coming more often now.

One thought twisting into ten,

Had to stay clean. Had to stay invisible.

They were closing in. I could feel it. Even if they did get close, I've taken precautions. They're always one step behind.

I moved every forty-eight hours. Motels. Airbnb aliases, so many I lost count. Hell, I slept in the back of a busted-out truck once, staring through rusted holes in the roof, wondering how long it would take the world to forget my name.

But they wouldn't. I'd make sure of it. Not as long as Lani was still out there smiling. Not while Myles was still breathing.

I stood up, started pacing. The walls in here were too close, too thin. They echoed every thought back at me, louder than before.

They deserve this.
They deserve this.
They deserve this.

"She doesn't get to forget me," I growled, slamming my fist into the drywall.

The crack it made was loud and sharp. The surprise of it felt like a gunshot in the quiet.

I flexed my fingers, ignoring the sting in my knuckles. "I gave her everything," I muttered. "She needed someone like me. Someone who would always take care of her."

But she couldn't see that in me. All she saw was Myles. She wanted soft. Safe. Predictable. She wanted him.

I laughed. A dry, hollow sound that didn't even touch my eyes. "You want safe, Lani? You'll get safe. I'll give you safe."

I peeled back the curtain just an inch and looked outside. The parking lot was still, silent. Silent.

Didn't mean anything.

They were out there. Watching. Tracking. Probably knew what hoodie I wore to grab coffee this morning. I should probably burn it. Probably had a file on every burner I'd touched. Probably traced that LLC ten steps back to me by now, or who they think I am.

But none of that mattered.

Because I still had time.

I still had her schedule memorized. Still knew which deliveries she dropped off herself and which ones she didn't. Knew Myles jogged three times a week, like clockwork, ever since he limped out of that hospital.

They thought the story had wrapped.

It hadn't even hit the middle yet.

"I see you," I murmured, tapping her frozen face on my screen. "And soon, you'll see me."

The bathroom light buzzed one final time, then died, plunging the room into darkness. The hum in the walls crawled across the ceiling like spiders.

And in the dark, I smiled.

Chapter 33

Lani

The sun had just begun to dip below the skyline, painting the evening in warm hues of orange and gold. A breeze fluttered through the Soul Music Festival, carrying the mingled scents of roasted peanuts, incense, and fragrant oils from food trucks and vendor stalls. The atmosphere was unmatched.

I moved through the crowd, my hair pulled up in a high puff wrapped in a vibrant headscarf. Loose-fitting denim overalls hung just right over a cropped top, and with every step, my sandals clinked softly against the artisan beaded jewelry draped at my waist, wrists, neck, and ankles. I felt like I belonged in a painting… vibrant and free.

When Myles spotted me, I knew instantly. His whole face lit up, pride in his eyes, and maybe something else. That look still made me feel giddy inside, just like the first day we met.

He walked toward me in fitted black pants and a dashiki that clung perfectly across his broad chest. The bold colors glowed under the string light, a striking change from his usual jeans and polo. I had to take a minute to fully appreciate this fine specimen. *My man, my man, my man.* Pride filled my eyes too, with a little lust thrown in for good measure.

"Okay…that looks good on you. I love a versatile man," I grinned as he approached.

"And you? You look like you walked out of a dream I once had."

He reached for my hand and gave it a gentle squeeze, then pulled me close and kissed my forehead.

"Ready to see what they have going on out here?"

"Let's go," I said, and just like that, we were swallowed by the rhythm of the night.

The music thumped low and sweet, wrapping around our chests and making everything else fall away. Spoken word artists poured out their souls, and dancers moved like living poems. It wasn't just a festival, it was freedom, culture, healing.

We laughed, swayed, browsed vendors, and shared fresh mango slices and jerk skewers. I couldn't stop smiling. Myles kept his arm loosely around my waist, anchoring me without caging me.

Then the DJ dropped Jill Scott's "He Loves Me," and everything slowed. The makeshift dance floor filled with couples. Myles turned to me, eyes soft and searching.

"Dance with me," he said.

I nodded, letting him pull me in close. We moved slowly, like the song was just for us. The crowd faded, the lights dimmed, and it was just the two of us.

I closed my eyes and leaned into his chest, feeling the beat of his heart.

Then I felt his lips graze my ear.

"I'm here... however long it takes. But I just want you to know..." his voice dropped. "I love you."

I froze.

My body stiffened, heart thundering in my chest.

He must've felt it.

I didn't move. Didn't say anything.

My mind spun out of control.

Why me? After Michael... after Darius... Can I even trust myself anymore? Myles has never taken from me. He's only given. He stayed. Even after the worst of it, he stayed. This man literally got shot because of me. What more proof do I need?

But the scars whispered louder than the logic.

Myles pulled back slightly, brushing a strand of hair from my cheek. "What's wrong? You okay?"

I looked up, and gave him a soft smile that didn't quite reach my eyes. "Nothing," I lied. "Just… a little chill in the air."

He didn't push. He just pulled me back into his arms, held me close, and let the music carry us.

Later, near the parking lot, the night winding down, he cupped my face, and kissed me again. No pressure or expectations.

"Goodnight, Love," he whispered against my forehead.

"Night, Babe."

I watched him walk away, fingers still tingling from his touch.

My car ride was too quiet. It led to my thoughts spinning.

"Damn," I muttered, gripping the steering wheel.

Should I have said it? Did I scare her off? Was it too soon?

I replayed the moment, how she tensed, how her smile dimmed.

"How can she not see I meant it?" I whispered.

I let the window down and turned the radio up, hoping the breeze and SiR's "D'Evils" might clear the doubt building in my chest.

"She's worth it," I said aloud. "Even if she's not ready. I'll wait."

City lights blinked across the windshield like flickering hopes I refused to let go.

I sat on the edge of my bed, phone in hand, thumb hovering.

My heart was a mess, but I knew I owed him a real conversation.

I took a deep breath and typed:

Me: Hey... I've been thinking. I need to talk to you. Can you meet me at Othello's for brunch tomorrow? 11?

Three dots appeared.

Myles: Of course. I'll be there.

I stared at his reply for a long moment, biting my lip before finally putting the phone down.

I tossed and turned, arms behind my head as I stared at the ceiling fan spinning above me.

"We need to talk," I murmured, quoting the text out loud.

The worst phrase in the English language.

Did I move too fast?

Should I have waited?

Is she pulling away now?

I tried music, TV, reading. Nothing helped.

Eventually, I gave up on sleep and just watched the sunrise paint gold across the walls, hoping the day wouldn't end with heartbreak.

The bell above the door jingled as I stepped into the cozy café. I was calm, but underneath, my heart was pounding.

Myles was already seated in the back booth, dressed in a denim shirt with the sleeves rolled up, a little tired around the eyes, but still managing a small smile when he saw me.

"Hey," he said, standing as I approached.

"Hey," I replied softly, sliding into the seat across from him.

We looked over the menu, neither of us really hungry, but it was something to do to avoid talking. I can't lie, the sweet smell of pancakes and freshly ground coffee did start to encourage me to order while we avoided eye contact.

Finally, I exhaled.

"When you said you love me… everything in me wanted to believe it. I really did." My fingers twisted the cloth napkin in my lap. "But my heart, my head, went into panic mode."

Myles stayed quiet, giving me space to finish.

"I started asking myself why. Why me? Why would this beautiful, brilliant man choose someone with the kind of history I have?" I looked up, eyes shimmering. "I've been lied to. Used. I lost pieces of myself with Michael… and with Darius, I'm not even sure what parts of me are real after all of that. And then here you come, patient, loving, consistent."

I paused, voice faltering.

"And I just keep wondering… what if I'm wrong again? What if this is just another one of life's cruel jokes. What if I fall, and this time there's no soft landing? I don't know if I can pick up the pieces like I did last time. I'm terrified."

Myles leaned in, and replied, his voice steady and warm. "Lani… I didn't say those words to scare you. I said them because I see you. All of you. The woman who's healed herself piece by piece. The woman who shows up for others even when she's running on empty. The one who shines, so bright, I'd still find her in the blackest blackout. I've loved you for a while, but just got the courage to tell you. I pray you can see it in my actions. You are deserving of everything I have to offer, and more."

I blinked, trying to hold it together.

"I don't want perfect," he continued. "I want you just the way you are. You are perfect for me. I'm not here to fix you, or save you. I just want to build and grow with you. If you need me, I am here to support you. There is no pressure or timeline. Just me and you, however long it takes."

My throat tightened. "Myles…"

He reached across the table and covered my hand with his. "I'll wait. I'll walk slowly. Just don't shut me out."

Silence settled between us, but this time it was warm, full of unspoken things finally said.

After a beat, I smiled, more like an evil grin. "You ever been roller skating?"

Myles raised a brow. "Not since I was ten and nearly broke my ass. I've been kind of scared."

I laughed. "Perfect. I can't skate at all. Let's do it."

Myles gave me the most incredulous look. "I love you, that is the only reason I am agreeing to this, remember that woman!"

The roller rink was alive with colored lights and old-school R&B. I clung to the wall, legs wobbling like a fresh-out-of-the-womb calf.

"Oh, this was a terrible idea," I laughed.

Myles, equally shaky, clung to the rail. "AGREED! I'm a grown-ass man out here looking like a baby giraffe."

"More like Bambi on ice," I teased, nearly falling. "Hold my hand!"

"Why, so we both can fall?" He laughed, but he reached for my hand anyway.

We bumped into each other, giggling like kids, stumbling across the polished floor.

"I'm not even skating. I'm just vibrating across the floor," he muttered.

"You're doing great," I said, breathless. "You only fell twice."

Eventually, we made it to the center of the rink, and just stood there, holding hands, catching our breath.

"You know," he said, eyes locking with mine, "if this is what falling looks like, I'm good with it."

I smiled, heart wide open. "Me too."

And under the slow burn of a love song, and the swirl of disco lights, we laughed until our faces hurt, two people figuring it out, one stumble at a time.

I curled deeper into the couch cushions, legs tucked beneath me as I nursed my second glass of red wine. A jazz playlist hummed in the background, soft saxophone notes weaving through the air like a lullaby. Sean sat cross-legged across from me, her face flushed with post-honeymoon glow, her braids piled high, and wild atop her head, laughter coming easily between sips.

"Girl, listen," she said, sloshing the wine in her glass. "Being a wife? I love it. I love it. I mean, it's not like everything's changed overnight, but waking up next to Carlos knowing he's my husband now? It hits different."

I grinned, soaking up her joy. "It's that official love. That I said it in front of God, and my mama, so you know it's real love."

"Exactly! Like, we already knew we were locked in, but now it feels rooted. Intentional. We're building something, you know? We've even talked about kids, maybe not right away, give it a year or two, but it's definitely on the table. I can't wait to have little chocolate, curly-haired babies running around, driving him crazy." She leaned forward. "And the sex? Let's just say... things got real creative."

We both laughed until my shoulders dropped, and I glanced down at my glass. "I'm happy for you, Sean. For real."

Sean's eyes narrowed. "But...?"

I hesitated. "Myles told me he loves me."

She squealed, nearly dropping her wine. "Wait, what? Like, said the words out loud for you to hear?"

"Yeah," I said with a half-smile. "He said it at the Soul Music Festival. We were dancing, and he just whispered it like it was nothing. Like he already knew."

Her hands flew to her mouth. "Girl, that man has been in love! I can't believe you are sitting here acting like you didn't know."

I let out a breath. "It just really caught me off guard."

"What?"

"I kind of froze. I mean, it was beautiful, but..." My voice drifted. "I got in my head, and started second-guessing everything."

Sean's excitement softened. "Talk to me."

"I thought about Michael, and Darius. About the damage they did, what I let them do. What I chose. And I started wondering if I even trust myself to know when something's real. I mean, what if I mess this up? What can I even offer him? He's such a good man, and he's been nothing but amazing to me. He even took a bullet because of my bad decision-making, and never uttered a word of blame."

Sean reached across the table and took my hand. "Lani. You're not the same woman who let Michael drain her, or who didn't see Darius for what he was right away. You've grown. You're wiser now. And most of all, you're not choosing from a place of brokenness anymore. You are a total baddie with a good heart. I don't want to hear any more of this talk about what you have to offer. You are more than enough, beautiful, successful, and have a great personality. Hell, if I weren't married and, you know, didn't like men, I'd be in there."

Tears welled in my eyes, whether from emotion or laughter, I couldn't say.

"You are enough," Sean said, squeezing my hand. "You're more than enough. You and Myles? Y'all complement each other. He's the yin to your yang. You're spontaneous where he's steady, equally yoked, or whatever the Bible says. That man sees your light, and not only does he love it, he wants to protect it. I hear him and Carlos on the phone talking. You are safe with that man."

I smiled. "Why are you always right? Well almost because you did root for Darius at first." I chuckled.

"*I mean...* we all make mistakes... but never mind that, don't you owe Carlos and me an apology slash thank you meal?"

I laughed. "I do. This Saturday?"

"Saturday," Sean agreed, raising her glass. "To real love and new beginnings."

We clinked glasses and let the wine do its job.

The sun cast long streaks of gold across the pavement as we settled into our corner patio table at The Grill, a new spot in downtown Stonebrook. The place was alive, waiters weaving through tables, drinks flowing, the smell of Cajun butter and smoked bacon wrapping itself around every conversation. I sat between Myles and Sean, my hand resting lightly on his thigh beneath the table.

Carlos broke the ice. "So when is it going to be y'all's turn? The way those speeches went at the wedding, I thought we would've heard something by now."

Myles spoke up before I could. "Slow your roll now. Can I tell the girl I love her for a solid week first? Dang."

Everyone laughed. I let myself sink into the comfort of the moment, into the safety of my tribe. Myles was being his usual charming self, exchanging jokes with Carlos. Sean was showing off honeymoon photos on her phone. It felt good. The four of us together just felt right.

It happened in the quickest moment between blinks. A chill slid down my spine, and goosebumps rose across my arms. Something in me shifted before I even knew why. I glanced around the crowd instinctively, feeling eyes on me, my heart tightening in my chest.

And then I saw him.

Across the parking lot, just past the first line of cars, stood Darius. Tall. Motionless. Eyes fixed.

Right on me.

My breath hitched. The laughter and clinking glasses around me faded under the heavy throb of my pulse.

He didn't move. Didn't blink. Just stared, his face a mask of hatred and malice.

I looked away fast, turning back to my plate, my heart rattling in my chest. Instinctively, I leaned into Myles, inherently drawn to the feeling of protection.

"Babe?" Myles's voice was soft and gentle. "You okay?"

I forced a smile. "Yeah. Just... I thought I saw someone I knew. But I'm good."

I didn't dare look again.

The second Myles left my apartment, I locked the door, shut every blind, and made my way straight to the living room. My hands were shaking as I dialed Detective Imere's private line. I gave him my name, praying he remembered me so I wouldn't have to tell the whole story again.

An hour later, he stood at my door, notepad in hand, his eyes sharp and focused.

"You're sure it was him?" he asked.

"Positive. He didn't say anything or come close. He just watched me. I didn't call right away because I didn't want to risk a scene if Myles saw him. After having Myles's shot, the last thing I wanted was for them to have a confrontation that could lead to him being hurt again. I figured calling from home after the fact would avoid all that, and you could still catch him on the security footage nearby."

Detective Imere nodded and scribbled in his notebook. "I'll work on it. I'm glad you called. Nothing new to report yet on my end, but I'll have patrols increased around your neighborhood. If he shows up again, don't hesitate. Day or night, you call. Next time, alert the police immediately. Discreetly excuse yourself if you need to, but we have to get this man off the street before he escalates further."

"Thank you," I said, hugging my arms around myself.

He paused at the door. "We'll catch him, Ms. Shields. Stay alert. But don't let him steal your peace."

When the door clicked shut behind him, I stood there for a long moment, leaning against it, eyes closed.

Not again.

Chapter 35

The hum of fluorescent lights and the low clang of metal filled the empty gym. It was too early for most, but for Myles and me, this time was sacred, midweek workouts before the world stirred.

I bent forward into a hamstring stretch, my fingers brushing my sneakers. My breath was steady, but my nerves weren't. I had to drag myself in here this morning because I hadn't slept much. The image of Darius's cold, unblinking stare from yesterday haunted every thought, every blink.

I glanced over at Myles, who stood beside me, rolling his shoulders and yawning through his warm-up.

"Hey," I said quietly.

He turned to me, a little smirk playing on his lips. "What's up, sleepyhead?"

"Yesterday, I know you felt something was off at one point during lunch. I said it was nothing, but...I saw Darius yesterday."

Myles froze and just stared at me in disbelief.

Silently, I stood up slowly, keeping my eyes on him, trying to read his reaction. "He was at The Grill. Across the parking lot. Just... standing there. Watching us."

Myles's jaw clenched. "And you didn't say anything?"

"I didn't want to ruin the mood with my drama," I said quickly. "I didn't want you to feel like you had to react, to protect me, or prove something. We were having fun and,"

"Fun?" His voice rose slightly. "Lani, what the hell? You saw him... and said nothing?"

I stepped closer, my voice trembling but firm. "I was afraid for you. I know you. I know how you operate. You'd have confronted him right then and there. And Darius is sick...he wants that. There is no doubt in my mind that you can protect me, but Darius is not well, we can't even imagine the lengths he would go. He'd love nothing more than to remove you from my life, be that by jail or in the grave. I can't lose you, Myles. I'm not letting him take anything else away from me. Especially not you! I have fought incredibly hard to fall in love and be happy, I have finally found that in you, and that bastard does not get to take you away from me. In any capacity, so yes, I withheld that information."

He stared at me in disbelief, chest heaving. I could hear his deep breaths trying to calm himself down. Then he looked away, pacing toward the weight bench before turning back.

"You're damn right I would've confronted him."He closed the distance between us in three long strides and stopped inches from me.

His eyes locked on mine, steady and burning with something primal. He firmly grabbed my chin so he could look me directly in the eyes.

"I'm your man, my job is to protect you. Mind, body, and spirit," he said, low and deliberate. "I take that role very seriously, Milani. I promise you, given the opportunity to rid you of having to deal with that bastard, I would put him in the dirt. I don't need you running interference trying to protect me. Let me protect us."

My breath hitched.

"Do you understand me?"

I nodded slowly, swallowing the tight knot in my throat.

Myles exhaled, trying to calm himself, but the fire in his eyes lingered. "I know you were trying to protect me. And maybe..."

his voice softened just a little, "maybe you're not used to a real man who cherishes you above all."

He placed a hand on my waist, grounding me."But that's what I am. I'm your man. You don't get to take that opportunity from me, Lani. You don't get to make that choice for both of us. We are a team, even through fear, we move together."

He dropped his voice to a reverent whisper. "Promise me you'll never do that again."

I blinked fast, my emotions rising. Guilt, fear, love, and a dangerous spark of desire all crashing into each other at once.

"I promise," I whispered.

"Good." He brushed my cheek with his thumb, then stepped back and nodded toward the bench press. "Now let's work off this anger. I do believe this was our first argument."

We finished the rest of our workout in intense silence, both focused but tethered tightly to one another. Every lift, every rep, every exchanged glance was loaded with unspoken weight.

After showering and changing, we grabbed smoothies and drove through Stonebrook's industrial district. The buildings were a blend of aging brick facades and sleek renovations, warehouses reborn as art galleries, breweries, and boutique fitness studios.

I held my phone up in selfie mode, live streaming to my growing followers.

"Alright y'all, I've been scouting spots because Posh Sweets is officially too big for my kitchen," I said, panning to a row of buildings with tall windows and exposed piping. "I've been thinking something like this, what do we think? Exposed brick? High ceilings? Y'all feeling the vibes?"

Myles, in the driver's seat, looked over and smirked "Tell them I'm already working on security upgrades for whichever one you pick."

I blinked at him in surprise, then smiled wide. "Y'all hear that? My man said he's making it a fortress for his queen. Isn't he, so sweet?"

The chat lit up instantly: "Ooooh is that him??" "Protective bae energy, YES." "We love a man who supports the dream."

Myles laughed under his breath but didn't turn away from the camera. He rested his hand casually on my thigh."Whatever she dreams, I build it stronger."

That wasn't just content. That was a statement. He said that with his whole chest, for me. *Swoon.*

We ended the night back at Myles's place, curled up on the couch, my feet tucked under his thigh, wine in my hand, popcorn between us.

Some action flick played on mute while we talked quietly.

"You kind of scared me for a moment there earlier," I said. "But I understand where your anger came from, and I apologize."

He rubbed my leg gently. "I know. I just needed you to understand how serious I was in that moment. How serious I am about you in general. I don't just tell you I love you because it sounds cute, and I want to show you that in every way possible. What I have for you is genuine, and I am prepared to protect it at all costs."

The way he stared into my eyes as he spoke sent every nerve in my body tingling with need. I shook myself, this was a serious moment, Lani, not the time to drift into the gutter. Instead of letting desire steal the weight of it, I whispered, "I have never felt more protected in my life. Thank you for that."

"That's the idea."

I leaned my head against his chest and let the quiet wrap around us. The storm wasn't over. Darius was still out there somewhere being a menace. But this moment, this peace, this man, it was all mine, and I would hold it as long as possible.

I sat at my desk, one hand cradling my phone, the other spinning my gold pen between my fingers. Morning sunlight spilled through the floor-to-ceiling windows of my office, catching on the sleek new "Partner" plaque mounted beside my name.

I took a breath.

Then I hit dial.

Carlos answered on the second ring. "Yo, what's good, man?"

"I need to meet. You and Sean."

There was a pause. Then I heard the grin in his voice. "This a surprise?"

I smirked, but kept my tone neutral. "Yeah. Something like that."

In the background, I heard him yell, "Hey baby! Myles is about to ask Lani to marry him, and he needs our help!"

My eyes widened. "Bruh."

Seconds later, Sean's voice cut through, high-pitched, and shrill, "OH MY GOD!!!"

I pinched the bridge of my nose, laughing despite myself.

"Now what if she had her on speaker? I would've kicked your ass for ruining my surprise."

Carlos chuckled. "Then it's a good thing she wasn't. Come on, we've all been waiting for you to stop playing and lock it down."

"Yeah, yeah. Can we just meet before Sean starts designing save-the-dates?"

"Tonight. Shades Lounge. Seven."

"Bet."

I hung up and leaned back in my chair, staring out over Stonebrook. My heart was steady, but my mind wouldn't stop racing.

This was it.

No more letting Darius haunt the corners of our happiness. No more shadows dictating how I moved. Lani had held me down, loved me with a kind of fire that softened the hardest parts of me. She was joy, grit, and peace all in one. My woman, my partner in every sense.

I was ready to put a ring on it. But more than that, I was ready to build her dream too. I wanted to give her everything those bastards took from her tenfold.

Later that evening, I pulled up to Shades Lounge, one of the places Carlos and I used to hit after class when we were in college. Spoken word buzzed through the building like electricity, the room lit in warm reds and deep shadows.

Sean greeted me with a hug, vibrating with excitement. "So?! Tell us everything! What's the plan, how are we doing this, do I need a dress?!"

Carlos shook his head. "Sean, breathe."

I leaned forward. "Alright. Here's the plan."

I pulled out a folded sketch of the industrial space Lani had been eyeing during her live stream.

"I'm buying her a building for her bakery."

Sean gasped. "You mean the one she's been dreaming about?!"

I nodded. "It's already in motion. Paperwork's getting finalized under an LLC I set up for her, that way she won't recognize it if she does look into it. I'm going to renovate it top to bottom, just how she wants it. She'll walk in, and everything will be ready."

Carlos let out a low whistle. "Okay, Daddy Warbucks. What do you need from us?"

"Carlos, you're on security. Top-tier everything, cameras, panic buttons, coded entry. She needs to feel safe. With everything with Darius, I don't want her to be afraid to be there by herself."

Carlos nodded, already in work mode. "Done."

"Sean," I said, "I need you to find out everything she wants in that space without tipping her off. Colors, layout, appliances. When it's ready, you're the one bringing her there."

Sean beamed. "What about the ring?"

"I already got it, platinum toi et moi, one side a pear-shaped diamond, and the other an emerald-cut emerald, 7 carats of opulence."

"Well damn." Both Sean and Carlos exclaimed.

Carlos crossed his arms, smiling. "You really out here trying to make me look bad, huh?"

I laughed. "No. I'm just trying to give her what she deserves."

The following weeks were a whirlwind.

I wasn't in court much anymore; my name carried weight now. Instead, I was out in the city, facilitating deals, checking progress on the renovation, keeping everything tight. Her online following was blowing up. People loved seeing us together. "Myles the Taste Tester" became a whole segment on her channel.

Still, she had no idea what I was building just for her.

She kept talking about investors, leasing spaces, maybe crowdfunding. She had no clue her dream bakery was already under construction, brick by brick, oven by oven.

The ring had been ready for weeks now. It was safely sitting in my safety deposit box at the bank. It was unique and precious, just like her.

Now the final details were falling into place. Carlos had the security system nearly done. Sean had vision boards and excuses lined up. Luckily, there were no structural renovations that had to be done. The building itself was nearly complete.

I stood outside, key in hand, staring up at the signless glass.

It wasn't just about proposing.

It was about building a life. I wanted her to have the space to grow and achieve the greatness I could feel inside of her. I was a total simp for this woman, and I couldn't possibly care less. I was right where I wanted to be with who I wanted to be with. Nothing could make me happier.

Chapter 37

I stood in front of the full-length mirror, robe loosely tied, fingers gliding across the fresh gloss on my lips. My skin glowed, the kind of glow that came from hours of pampering, and laughter with my best friend, and not a single worry in sight. I tilted my head, inspecting the soft shimmer on my cheekbone. Sean popped her head into the room. "Okay, Miss Birthday Girl. Time to pick out your outfit for tonight."

I smirked. "I already told you I was wearing that green two-piece with the,"

"Absolutely not." Sean waved a manicured finger. "Tonight calls for elegance. After-six attire. Trust me."

I rolled my eyes, but smiled. "You've been really controlling today. I thought this was my birthday?"

Sean gasped with mock offense. "Girl, please. I just spent six hours in a spa listening to you complain about how your curls never act right, and how Myles drinks out the orange juice carton. Don't play me."

I laughed, giving in, as Sean pulled out a form-fitting, asymmetrical off-the-shoulder emerald green chiffon gown, the epitome classy with just enough sexiness.

"Oh," I breathed, touching the fabric. "That's…"

"Exactly it," Sean finished. "Put it on. I'll do your hair."

By the time the sun dipped behind the skyline, I was a vision. My hair swept into an elegant chignon with a twist and cascading curls, the dress hugging my curves just right, skin glowing like the goddess I was.

We walked out of the salon with shopping bags in hand, and Sean jingled the keys. "You driving?"

I shrugged. "I thought you said you were driving?"

"I was, but if you really want to."

"Sean. Be so for real right now. You just said yesterday I couldn't drive if my life depended on it."

Sean feigned deep thought.

"That's true... and I kinda want to live long enough to have those little curly-haired babies I told you about."

I laughed, sliding into the passenger seat. After all, it was my birthday, passenger princess me please.

"You're a mess," I said through my laughter.

We were halfway through Stonebrook when I narrowed my eyes. "Okay... where are we going exactly?"

Sean didn't flinch. She just turned up the volume on the music and hummed along to the beat.

"Sean."

"Hmm?"

"You got quiet. That means you're hiding something." Sean grinned, her eyes on the road.

"Girl, you are paranoid. It's your birthday. You said you wanted good food and a vibe. I'm delivering."

I crossed my arms, glancing out the window as the scenery began to shift, less nightlife, more industrial buildings, warehouses, and commercial zones. My stomach fluttered.

"Okay, but why are we in Stonebrook's industrial district now? You taking me to some underground speakeasy or something?" Sean simply smiled and hit the turn signal."Sean."

"Trust me."

My heart picked up. My eyes scanned the street, my breath short.

We turned the corner and slowed in front of a sleek, newly renovated brick building. The exterior was minimalist but beautiful, with black awnings and warm sconces casting soft light across a frosted glass door. Painted in delicate white script across the top panel: Posh Sweets. My name. My body froze. I couldn't breathe. My voice caught. "What... what is this?"

Sean cut the engine, stepped out, and walked around to my door. "Come on," she said softly, extending a hand. I stared at the building. My dream. But how? I hadn't even applied for funding yet. I hadn't submitted any offers. The LLC wasn't even official yet.

"Sean, what is this?"

"Just follow me."

My legs moved before my brain caught up. My heels clicked against the pavement. My hand trembled in Sean's. My chest heaved. My mind raced. Was this a birthday prank? A pop-up? Did someone lease the space and steal my name?

As we reached the door, Sean reached into her clutch and pulled out a silver key. She handed it to me. "You open it."

I stared at the key. Then back at her. Sean smiled.

"Happy birthday, sis."

With shaking fingers, I slid the key into the lock and turned. The door opened into a warm, glowing space. Twinkling lights strung from rustic beams above. Marble counters and glass bakery cases gleamed under pendant lighting. Soft jazz music played in the background. The air smelled faintly of vanilla and cinnamon. And at the center of it all, standing beneath a floral arch, was Myles. In a slate gray suit, a single red rose in hand.

My knees buckled slightly. He stepped forward, eyes locked on mine, voice steady.

"Happy birthday, baby."

My lips parted, but no words came. He took my hand.

"I didn't just want to give you a ring, Lani. I wanted to give you a foundation. A home for your dream. A space to build everything you've imagined. You've given me peace, love, purpose, us. This... is just the beginning."

He dropped to one knee and opened a velvet box. A brilliant emerald and diamond toi et moi sparkled back at me.

"Milani Aunjunae Shields... will you marry me?"

Tears spilled down my cheeks, and my hand flew to my chest as my breath hitched. "Yes," I whispered. Then louder through tears. "Yes! Of course I will!"

Myles stood, sliding the ring onto my finger before pulling me into his arms. The kiss that followed was electric, years of struggle, healing, and growth folded into a single moment. Sean and Carlos clapped from behind.

Sean was already crying. "About damn time!"

Later, Myles and I stood alone inside the bakery, arms wrapped around each other as I walked the floor, taking it all in.

"I can't believe you did this," I whispered.

"I told you," he murmured into my hair. "Forever starts now. I'm not letting anyone dictate our story."

I nodded, overwhelmed. "This is everything. I love you."

He pulled back, eyes soft. "You're my everything, I love you more than life itself. The only thing I can even think I could love as much as you is our bad-ass kids whenever we decide to have them."

That earned him a playful smack on the arm, followed by sweet kisses interrupted by giggles.

"My kids won't be bad!" I chided.

The ride home was filled with so much anticipation that we both were uncharacteristically quiet. I was in my head wondering how I got so lucky with this man of mine. He not only asked me for my forever, he provided the foundation for my dream. I could love on him for the rest of my life, and it still would not accurately articulate what I feel for him in this moment.

As we entered his apartment, the door clicked shut behind us, and suddenly the place felt different. Like it had shifted into something sacred, something ours. We were not just two single people anymore, we had promised each other a future together. The silence wrapped around us, but it wasn't empty. It was thick with anticipation fueling our desires and need.

I turned to look at him, my husband-to-be. Myles was already watching me like I'd hung the stars. His gaze flickered to my ring, then back to my face, and before I could speak, his mouth was on mine, warm and tender at first. I could taste the sweet fruity notes of the champagne as our tongues danced.

"You said yes," he breathed against my lips, like he still couldn't believe it.

"I did," I whispered, tasting his relief, his want, his joy, feeling his smile in the kiss that followed.

He kissed me like the world had stopped. Like I was the only thing anchoring him to this moment. I felt it too, the rightness of it all. His hands moved down my back, firm and familiar, pulling me flush against him. So close I could feel his heartbeat against my chest. So close I could feel his desire for me. I could feel the heat rising between us, slow and steady, like a storm building languidly beneath the surface, promising raw ecstasy and passion.

I slid his jacket off his shoulders, letting it fall to the floor. My dress suddenly felt too tight. Myles's strong hands found the tiny zipper, releasing me while trailing soft kisses along my jaw and down my neck. I wanted skin. I wanted closeness. I wanted him, to feel his hands everywhere all at once. I burned for him, for the friction and the pressure needed to release me. But Myles took his time. Moving slowly, teasing every nerve in my body until I was wound tight as a guitar string.

Myles paused, his forehead resting against mine. His breath was uneven, his eyes full of reverence. "I've imagined this moment more times than I can count," he murmured.

I touched his face, tracing the line of his jaw with my thumb. "I hope it lives up to the hype, because I'm not going anywhere," I said, and meant it with every piece of me. "You're stuck with me."

A crooked smile tugged at his lips. "Good," he said, then scooped me into his arms before I could say another word.

I let out a startled laugh, wrapping my arms around his neck. "Myles..."

"Hush," he said against my throat, his lips brushing the sensitive skin just below my ear. "Let me have this."

Every step he took towards the bedroom sent shivers down my spine. By the time we reached the bedroom, I was aching in places that had nothing to do with lust, and everything to do with love.

He set me down gently, like I was breakable, but the way he looked at me said I was anything but. His gaze greedily devoured me as I lay there for him on display in next to nothing. Myles moved slowly, brushing my curls out of my face, studying me like he was memorizing every line. His kisses came next, feather light at first, down the side of my neck, across my shoulder. His lips and hands found every peak and valley my body had to offer.

"I could dream a thousand dreams, and nothing would ever be as perfect as this moment with you right now," he whispered, and something in me cracked wide open.

I pressed my hand to his chest, feeling his heartbeat thundering beneath my fingers. "Then love me, so we both know it's real," I said.

And he did.

Not in a rush. Not like he was trying to claim me. But like he already had, and now, he was cherishing what was his. Every kiss, moan, and caress was a promise. Every touch was a thread weaving us tighter, an impenetrable bond connecting not just our bodies, but our minds, souls, and hearts. And in that moment, with him, I felt more than just wanted. I felt complete.

Chapter 38

unlight spilled through the sheer curtains, casting shimmering pale yellow light across the bedroom. I stirred beneath the covers, stretching lazily as a contented yawn escaped my lips. I extended my left hand above my head, fingers splayed, the morning light catching my new engagement ring and scattering tiny rainbows across the ceiling. I smiled. A big goofy grin. Still sleepy, and disbelieving of the night we had.

"Still staring at it?" Myles's voice was low, rough with sleep, and amusement.

I rolled over to face him. "You gave me a whole bakery and a diamond. You expect me not to stare?"

He chuckled, tugging me close. "You're not mad I didn't really plan a weekend getaway?"

"Nope," I said, pressing a kiss to his lips. "Now I get to spend the weekend being a fiancé! I've got to break in my new title."

"Oh God," he groaned playfully. "Should I brace myself?"

"Yes," I said, beaming. "You absolutely should."

We kissed again, soft and slow, until I sighed and flopped onto my back.

"What's on your agenda today, fiancé?" I teased.

Myles grinned. "Gotta check in at the office. I've got a couple of contracts to look over, and a lunch meeting with a potential client. You?"

"Editing footage from yesterday." I stretched again. "I went live while Sean and I were doing birthday prep, and the stream numbers were crazy. It hit a record."

"Of course it did. You're magnetic."

He kissed my cheek.

"I'll try not to get jealous that you're more famous than me." He replied with a smile.

I grinned. "Oh please, half my comments were like 'Where's your man?' and 'Does he have a brother'? I should've put your face behind a paywall."

He smirked. "It's not too late."

We got out of bed and readied for the day. I packed my camera and laptop while Myles slipped into his tailored slacks and button-down. We moved with ease, the rhythm of a couple fully in sync.

Before I left, he caught me by the hand at the door. "Hey, you're meeting Sean and Carlos at the bakery at seven, correct? I can bring wine and make it a thing."

"That will be perfect, and yes, seven is correct," I replied.

Myles kissed my knuckles. "Perfect. We'll make it a party."

Back at my apartment, I was curled up on the couch, footage pulled up on my laptop, fingers flying across the keyboard as I edited. My ring caught the light each time I adjusted the video timeline. I was halfway through trimming when something strange caught my eye. An odd blur in the lower corner of the screen, barely noticeable at first. A shadow. It wasn't shaped like any of the staff or equipment. I paused the footage, zooming in. The shadow was stretched, distorted by angle and lighting, but it looked like someone standing just out of frame. Watching. My brow furrowed. I rewound. Played it again. Paused. Still nothing I could make out clearly. Could've been a trick of the light or someone walking past. But my gut twisted, uneasy. Don't jump to conclusions, I told myself, brushing the chill off my arms. I shook it off and finished the edit.

The proposal video went live at one that afternoon, and within fifteen minutes my phone exploded. Comments rolled in nonstop.

"This is the best proposal I've ever seen."

"Okay, but WHERE do I find a Myles?"

"They got that on Amazon?"

"Ma'am. Drop the registry link. I need to support this level of excellence."

"Does Myles have a cousin? A play cousin? A neighbor?"

I laughed, so hard I snorted. Yesterday I'd been on cloud nine. Today? I was somewhere in the stratosphere.

That evening, Myles arrived first, holding a bottle of red in one hand and a bag of my favorite dish in his other. I was mid-live stream when I saw him come in.

"Alright y'all," I said to the camera, turning toward the door with a huge smile. "Say hey to the groom-to-be!" Myles stepped into frame like a natural.

"Hey everyone. I'm Myles. Groom-to-be. Official taste tester. Future baby daddy."

I gasped, fake punched him in the chest. "Sir!"

He staggered dramatically, clutching his heart. "Ow! She hits me, y'all. Pray for me."

The comments exploded.

"These two are GOALS."

"Future baby daddy?! Okayyy!"

"We stan a theatrical king."

"They are just too stinkin' cute!"

Sean and Carlos came in moments later, waving at the camera. Sean leaned into frame. "I'm Sean, matron of honor, moral compass, and the person who made sure this proposal didn't involve Myles in a tuxedo holding balloons outside her apartment window."

Carlos added with a grin, "Carlos. Best man. Security detail. IT genius, one and only husband to the matron of honor, and all-around party animal."

Everyone fell out laughing. Once the introductions wrapped, I ended the live stream and collapsed into a chair.

"That was ridiculous," I laughed. "But I love us."

Carlos got straight to business, pulling up the digital schematics. "Alright, so here's the layout. Cameras at every entrance, motion sensors near windows. You'll get real-time alerts to your phone, and here's the panel for arming and disarming the alarm."

I followed him as he walked through the functions, my brow raised in appreciation.

"This is high-tech as hell," I said.

Carlos winked. "Only the best for Posh Sweets. Not to mention I had to get into your fiancé's pockets."

Myles laughed. "That's my baby right there. I'm paying whatever...twice if I have to."

Sean, meanwhile, was unpacking a grocery bag and sliding ingredients across the counter.

"What are you doing?" I asked.

Sean looked at me innocently. "It's time for your first official pastry in the new space."

"Oh no," I groaned. "Can't we just say we did and don't?"

"I bought everything," Sean said, triumphantly holding up a bag of flour. "We're making honey buns. Non-negotiable."

"I am not baking under pressure," I protested, already tying on an apron.

"You are," Sean said, handing me a whisk. "This is your warm-up."

The smell of cinnamon and sugar soon filled the space, rich and nostalgic. As the honey buns baked, I leaned on the counter, fingers sticky with glaze, laughter echoing around me.

It was then that Sean cleared her throat dramatically.

"Best friend," she began, voice sweet and sly. "You're not the only one with a bun in the oven."

I blinked. "I mean, yeah. Literally, you helped. We just put a dozen in there."

Sean stared at me. Carlos grinned. Myles's eyes went wide. My brows pulled together in confusion. "Wait, what?"

And then it clicked. My jaw dropped. My hands flew to my mouth. "SHUT UP."

Sean nodded, tears already brimming. "We're pregnant."

The scream I let out could've shattered glass. I rushed around the island and wrapped Sean in the tightest hug imaginable. Both of us were crying and laughing as Carlos and Myles clapped and dapped each other up in the background. Joy filled the room like rising dough, warm, full, unstoppable. Twelve buns in the oven, plus one. I just basked in the joy, and the favor placed upon me, and my circle. Absolutely nothing could steal the joy of this moment.

Chapter 39

Myles

The partners were still smiling when I left the conference room, their voices trailing behind me like echoes I couldn't shake.

"Myles, Atlanta's just the beginning. This puts you on a national stage."

I told them I'd think about it. Just a couple of days. That was the smart move, right? Buy time.

Breathe.

But my stomach hadn't unclenched since.

Now I stood in the produce aisle at the grocery store, watching Lani hold up two bunches of parsley like she was weighing the fate of the free world. One brow was arched. Her lips were pursed in playful debate. Any other day, I'd have kissed her beautiful full lips just to watch her pretend to be annoyed. Or to claim her for the world to see, to show how lucky I really am to have her at my side.

But today?

Today, I was distracted. This was a big move, but one I knew could make a big impact on my life in a professional aspect as well as personal. My proposal was still fresh. I knew Lani was the one. I would rather lose everything I have built than to ruin the life we have planned together.

I reached for a bag of apples I didn't need.

Lani glanced over. "You okay? You've been quiet since you got home."

"I'm good. Just thinking."

She tilted her head. "Thinking about what?"

I shrugged. "Nothing."

She blinked. Paused. Something shifted in her eyes, like she knew I was lying. "Okay," she said, but her voice had changed, cooler. "I'll go grab ginger."

That was a gift, and a curse with Lani. She was like me in a sense. She would not argue. She respected my boundaries a little too much sometimes. This time, she gave me enough room to hang myself by not pushing and prying further. My mind continued to weigh the pros and cons of the decision I was forced to make. This opportunity would be more money, more security for our family. The connections that I could make could open more doors and opportunities not only for me but for our future children as well.

At the end of this, the fact remained that I thought I would be with Shonda forever, but my ambition ruined that. I was more terrified than anything that I would make that same mistake with Lani. If I fumbled Lani due to working and neglecting her, I would not be able to live with myself.

We didn't talk much the rest of the trip. I cracked a joke in the checkout line. She smiled, but it didn't reach her eyes.

By the time we got back to the car, a quiet had settled between us that I didn't know how to break.

Lani drove. She didn't wait for me to speak, she just turned on the music.

She didn't need to say it. I could feel the wall rising between us. One brick at a time.

And the worst part?

I was the one laying the foundation.

Because I couldn't tell her the truth. Not yet.

Not when the last time I let ambition lead, it cost me everything. I didn't want Lani to try to sacrifice her happiness because she doesn't want me to miss out on an opportunity.

The next morning, I walked into the firm with a weight on my chest. I called a meeting with the partners and did my best to keep the tone light at the start. We exchanged small talk, joked about the last golf outing, and nursed lukewarm coffee in sleek, overpriced mugs.

Then I dropped the news.

"I appreciate the opportunity," I began, looking each of them in the eye, "but I have to decline the offer to lead the expansion to Atlanta. It's just not the right time for me, personally."

They were quiet for a moment. I could see the disappointment settle in, like they'd already envisioned the office opening, ribbon cutting, and press interviews with me front and center.

"Are you sure, Myles?" David asked. "We were hoping to get someone with a fresh perspective. Someone younger."

"I understand," I said, keeping my voice even. "That's why I think Seth should take the lead. He's got the experience, and he's already navigated the transition of a long-distance move. He'd be a great fit."

They nodded slowly, still digesting. I could tell they were holding out hope I'd change my mind, but they were already preparing to move forward with Seth if I didn't.

When the meeting ended, I exhaled, feeling relieved. I headed back to my office, finally able to concentrate on work, now that the weight had been lifted from my shoulders.

As I returned from lunch, Adrienne, my assistant, stopped me before I could step into my office. "Hey, just, so you know... Lani called."

I raised an eyebrow. "Everything okay?"

Adrienne gave me a look that was both apologetic and unsure. "I... might've let it slip that I was happy you weren't moving to Atlanta after all. I also congratulated her on the bakery, too. I thought she knew about the expansion, but it kind of became clear that she didn't. It was too late once I started. I couldn't just not answer her questions." She grimaced.

My stomach sank.

The personal nature of their conversation didn't bother me; Lani was like that. She could make anyone feel like they were best friends in one conversation. But her finding out about the expansion and that I turned it down from someone else? That wasn't going to go over well.

I gave Adrienne a tight smile and a nod. "Thanks for the heads-up." My tone said what I didn't, don't do that again.

I wrapped up work as quickly as I could and headed home, bracing myself.

When I walked into the apartment, I was greeted by the smell of sugar and vanilla, and the sound of Lani's voice, warm and animated.

She was live, baking her newest creation, Double Chocolate Macadamia Nut cookies. Her curls were pinned back, apron tied around her waist, her hands expertly moving between bowls and mixing spoons. I hovered just outside of frame, stealing a kiss on her cheek and peeking at the comments pouring in. Of course, her audience was drooling. My fiancé was stunning, creative, and magnetic.

But the moment I pulled back, I felt it.

Cool as ice.

She didn't miss a beat for the camera, though. Lani was locked in, her smile flawless. She wrapped up the live seamlessly once the cookies were out of the oven.

Then she turned on me.

"Oh, so now you want to be lovey-dovey?" she said, one brow arched.

I sighed. "Lani,"

"Don't Lani me," she snapped. "You made a major life decision for both of us and didn't even think to mention it? I had to hear it from Adrienne."

I rubbed the back of my neck. "I didn't mean for you to find out like that."

"It doesn't seem like you meant for me to know at all." Her voice was quieter now, but more pointed.

"I thought I was doing what was best for us," I admitted. "I was trying to protect what we're building. I've been down this road before, career first, relationship second. I didn't want to risk that again."

"I'm not Shonda," she said flatly. "And I'm not fragile. You could've brought it to me. I'm supposed to be your partner, remember. Or am I just the fiancé who decorates and bakes?"

"That's not fair,"

"It's how it feels. Is this not the same exact thing you asked me not to do? What happened to us moving together?"

She didn't yell. She didn't cry. She just walked past me, pausing at the hallway.

"I need space right now. Don't come ask me what's wrong. Don't follow me. You can stay, but you need to sleep in the guest room. If that doesn't work for you, you can always go back to your apartment. If you can't trust me with the hard stuff, how am I supposed to trust I have a voice in this relationship?"

Then she was gone.

And I was left alone, standing in the kitchen, the scent of cookies and regret thick in the air.

Lani's silent treatment lasted a full four days, and I'll admit, it was killing me. Not being able to snuggle up to her at night? Torture. Of course, she kicked me to the guest room. There was no breakfast waiting for me in the morning, no one to decompress with after a long day. It was hell.

People joke like the silent treatment is a blessing, peace, and quiet, right? Not for me. I missed my best friend. The cold shoulder from Lani was next level. As sweet and warm as she could be, when that fire turned icy, it burned just the same.

By day three, I had to call in the big guns: Carlos and Sean. Well, technically, I called Carlos to ask Sean to help a brother out. Of course, her best friend knew exactly what to say. Deep down, I already knew the answer, I just needed to hear it from someone else.

So on day four, I got up early, made her breakfast, checked her schedule, and did her morning prep. I wanted to make sure there were no excuses. No "this isn't a good time," no distractions. I needed to make this right.

When she finally walked into the kitchen, hair tied up, hoodie hanging off one shoulder, I handed her a cup of coffee and started talking.

"Lani, I'm sorry," I said, my voice low and sincere. "I never meant to make you feel like you weren't part of the team. That you weren't my partner. I love you more than anything. And I know you love me, so much that you'd probably try to sacrifice your dream for mine if it came down to it."

She didn't say anything, just stared into her mug. So I kept going.

"I know you. You give so much of yourself to everybody. I wanted to be the one supporting you this time. I didn't want you to feel guilty about me turning down the opportunity, because at the end of the day, none of that matters to me if I don't have you. You're what's important. As long as I can take care of us, we're good. I don't need the accolades. I don't need the extra responsibility."

I reached out and pulled her into me.

"Not to mention," I added, raising a brow and lowering my voice playfully. "I'm trying to work on expanding my legacy. Preferably tonight. You free?"

I wiggled my eyebrows like a clown, and that finally cracked her.

"You are such a cornball," she said, rolling her eyes, but smiling anyway.

"I love you, Myles," she said softly. "I just want to make sure we're on the same page before we get married. I'm not going to be just some housewife with no voice in this. My opinion matters. And if I ever feel like it doesn't, I'm out. If I have to remind you that I matter, we're already too far gone. After Michael, I promised myself I would never be voiceless again. I won't suffer in silence."

I nodded, pulling her even closer. "I understand. It won't happen again. Now can we please get back in bed? I've gone four days without spooning, and I'm going through withdrawals."

"It better not happen again because if it does, it's off to the guest room you go."

"You know I love you, but say 'guest room' one more time, and see what happens."

She laughed, and I didn't waste a second. I scooped her up, and marched her right back to bed, where I assumed my rightful place wrapped around her like a human blanket.

We spent the rest of the morning in bliss, cuddled up, and forgetting the world, until reality came knocking, and pulled us back into our responsibilities.

I've been hiding out in cash-only motels for the last few weeks. Moving constantly. The city's rhythm doesn't change much, but I do. No permanent address, no familiar places, just the anonymity of burner phones and the hum of a life lived behind the veil.

The one thing that remains constant is Lani. She's been smarter than I expected. Never showing her exact locations live, always posting delayed updates. She's so damn careful when she does go live, making sure to keep the surroundings vague, distant, never letting me get too close. But I can still feel her. Her presence. The way she holds herself in those posts, there's a distance, a shift. She's missing something. Me.

She and Myles... that asshole keeps showing up. Making himself known everywhere. I can't stand it. He thinks he's got some hold on her, like she'll just forget everything. But I can tell she's confused. I can feel it. She's not the same.

I've been patient, watching. I know she'll come back to me, it's only a matter of time. She needs me. I can free her from whatever grip he has on her. He thinks he's playing this smart, drawing up that lawsuit, but what he doesn't know? It's laughable. I control everything. None of my holdings are in my legal name. They don't even know my legal name. I am a ghost. They're too blind to see that.

Lani's got a big announcement coming up at one this afternoon. I have to be ready. This could be it, the moment she decides to let the world know the truth. Maybe, just maybe, she'll introduce me to her followers. Her real man.

One o'clock comes around, and I'm already on edge. I've been tracking her every move, waiting for her announcement to break.

But instead, it's a fucking proposal.

My mind races. What the hell is she doing? What's happening? This wasn't supposed to be it. My world tilts, and anger boils inside me. How dare he take that from me? How dare he ruin everything? I smash my fist into the wall of the hotel room, rage erupting like a volcano.

I tear the room apart. I don't care anymore. The dingy walls, the miserable surroundings, they don't matter. I rip the mirror off the wall. My reflection shattered, just like the reality of this whole situation. I tear the phone from the wall, hurling it to the ground, hearing the satisfying crack of plastic and glass. My breathing's ragged, my thoughts incoherent.

I grab the nearest beer bottle and throw it at the TV screen. The glass shatters with a sharp, metallic ring. Every sound of destruction is a release, a tiny piece of me unraveling with every violent motion. I'm past the point of control now.

And then, just like that, the anger ebbs. I stand there, surrounded by the wreckage, my pulse still racing. It's quiet for a moment. The weight of it all sinks in.

I don't care. I'll show her. I'll show everyone.

This is just the beginning. I'll give her something better than that pathetic bakery. Revenge. I'll give her revenge, something Myles's old, square ass will never be able to provide her. And as for me? I'm taking something back, too. After all, he's the reason Lani's judgment is clouded. He took her from me, so in a way, I'm the one who truly owns her now. She's mine. Always has been.

She'll see it soon enough. I'll make sure of it.

***

I watched him for three weeks.

The bane of my existence, toxic parasite, still up to the same old game. Different city, different woman, same playbook. I knew every step. Charm. Manipulate. Control. Drain. Leave them hollow. He hadn't changed.

I wonder if she knows about this other girl, Kayla? Kara? Something with a K. She almost looked just like Lani on the surface, but she could never in a million years compare to my angel. She lacked strength and confidence. It was crazy; he once had a precious jewel in his possession, and he treated her like she was nothing. The universe granted him a do-over, and he still acts the same…a real example of insanity. The same soft curls, the same dimples, the same wide, trusting eyes. She clung to his arm like he was some kind of savior. While he treated her like castaway trash.

Such a small, little man does not deserve to live. I wanted to scream at her. Scream at her to be better, to think better of herself, shake her, maybe shake the life out of her for being inadequate, take something from him because he took something from me. Her existence is futile either way. I can tell from the many bruises he's left on her body that she unsuccessfully tries to hide. This wasn't about her, though.

It was about him.

He ruined Lani. Broke something in her. Something that should've been mine to protect. If he hadn't gutted her with that betrayal of trust, maybe she would've seen me. Chosen me. She would have been ready for me and my intensity when I came along. Instead, she ran right into lover boy's arms like he was some damn Prince fucking Charming out of a fairy tale.

But I could fix it.

I will gift her this worthless bag of filth and get my hands dirty so she knows how deep my love for her goes. I will pay any cost including my soul for her happiness.

I sat outside his apartment in a stolen van. A plain white rusty work van. The type of vehicle that wouldn't warrant a second look. Stolen plates. But it didn't matter. This was a deceleration... She would know this was me. The cameras on the corner, I saw them, but I didn't care. If it came to that, I'd take the fall a thousand times for my precious love.

He stepped out of the building at 10:47 p.m. Sharp. Like he always did. Same khaki joggers, hoodie, and cocky-ass smirk. Probably heading to Kayla-Kara's whatever the fuck her name is place to mooch off or to knock her head between the washer and the dryer. Who knows, I don't bother trying to understand filth.

I stepped out, hoodie pulled low, gun already in hand.

"Yo," I said.

He paused, confused. "Do I know you?"

"Not yet." I raised the pistol and slammed it hard across his face. His hands shot up.

"Yo, hey, hey, man, take the wallet. You can have whatever."

"Shut up. I don't want your empty-ass wallet." I jammed the muzzle into his throat, trigger finger itching.

I had to calm myself because I needed to do this right for maximum effect. I shoved him toward the van. "Move, mother fucker."

He hesitated.

I cocked the gun.

That got him going. I took the zip-tie handcuffs from my back pocket and threw them at him. With the gun trained on the middle of his forehead, I growled through clenched teeth,"Put them on."

I watched him slip them on and pull the slack tight with his teeth.

I didn't speak on the drive. He begged. Whimpered. Offered money he didn't have. Said he had a girlfriend and a child, all shit I didn't care about. His sorry excuse of a life just further fueled my anger.

The warehouse sat like a rotting corpse beside the river. Quiet and forgotten, this place hadn't seen a visitor in years, which was exactly what I needed. The kind of place where people could scream for hours and no one would hear.

Inside, I tied him to a rusted chair, duct tape tight around his ankles. He screamed through the gag. I didn't care.

Let him scream.

I circled him, heart pounding. "You know why you're here?"

His eyes bulged. He shook his head, tears already spilling.

"Lani." I said forcefully spit flying from my mouth in the process.

That name hit like a slap.

"You broke her," I hissed. "You took something from her I can't get back. You made her doubt herself. You. You rerouted her whole life. And because of that, she ran from me. YOU PREVENTED HER FROM LOVING ME!" I screamed.

He mumbled something through the gag, still I didn't bother pulling it off.

I hit him.

Once.

Twice.

Again.

Fists, then the crowbar to the face.

Knuckles bruised. Blood sprayed.

Still I kept going until my frustration was evident by the look of his mangled body.

"You think women are disposable, huh? You think you get to leave scars and walk away?"

His breathing rattled. Head lulled to the side.

"Lani was supposed to be mine. You understand that? But no. You ruined her. So now, I have to make it right."

I leaned in close, forehead to his.

"This is the gift I'm giving her. Closure. Justice. Love. On our wedding day, she'll know I did this for her. She'll finally see me."

He was still. Barely breathing.

Pathetic filth.

I stood back, raised the gun, and didn't hesitate.

It sounded like a series of explosions, as I emptied the whole clip. Nothing less than what he deserved.

His body shook from the impact of the bullets, then slumped, immediately after the sound was swallowed by the warehouse walls.

I dragged him out the back to the river, wrapped in a tarp. Heavy. But not heavy enough to stop me. I dumped him in the river without a word. I gave him no more thought than that of discarded trash.

Gone.

It was done.

I stood on the shore, watching the ripples fade. Breathing hard. Smiling.

"For you, Lani, I'd send ten more worthless pieces of shit like him to meet their maker," I whispered. "Now we can begin."

She'd understand this message.

She'd have to.

Chapter 41

Genevieve, I swear to God, if you send me one more color swatch!" I yanked off my gloves, smearing buttercream across the edge of the prep table. My phone buzzed again, and sure enough, there it was.

Genevieve: Blush, or mauve? Thoughts, my darling?

I groaned loud enough to startle the delivery guy at the front of the bakery. "What's the difference?! They both look like freakin' pink!"

Sean, sitting on a stool in the corner with her feet propped up and one hand on her nonexistent baby bump, smirked at me. "They're completely different. One's romantic. The other says desperate bridesmaid."

I shot her a look. "You're really going to milk the hell out of this pregnancy, aren't you? For goodness sake, Sean, the bump ain't even bumpin' yet, and you're already being difficult."

"You know it, love," she said with a grin, clearly enjoying herself. "You love me, though, so it doesn't even matter."

I rolled my eyes. "I tell you, between you and Genevieve, I don't know who's worse. And I promise you, if I have to settle one more dispute between you two, there's gonna be trouble, trouble, trouble," I broke into a Bernie Mac impression for emphasis.

Sean grinned, totally unapologetic. "I need to keep the chaos minimal. For the baby." She patted her belly and leaned back, as if invoking some kind of maternal authority.

"You say that now, but remember it when you are going toe to toe with my wedding planner."

"I don't know why you hired her. We can totally do this together. Best friend bonding time."

"I know you are not trying to be jealous right now, Sean."

"Maybe a little," she squinted and gestured just a little bit.

"Oh my God," I groaned, feeling the weight of it all. "I'm not just planning a wedding, I'm parenting two women who think this is one of those bad reality TV shows."

By the time I got home, every nerve in my body was frazzled. As soon as I hit the living room, I collapsed onto the couch beside Myles, my safe place in human form.

He looked at me with a soft smile. "I take it Sean is still being Sean? Let me guess, she and Genevieve are still butting heads?"

I sank into the cushions and took the glass of wine he handed me. I sipped deeply. My eyes fluttered shut. "She's thorough, I'll give her that. But if I have to referee another creative difference between her and Sean, I'm going to plan my own elopement and live stream it from Vegas."

Myles chuckled, while he rubbed my feet, which were currently propped on his lap. "Is there anything I can do?"

"No," I pouted. "You just keep being perfect. That's your job."

He grinned, leaning over to kiss my nose. "Don't forget you have to take me to the airport tomorrow morning. I've got that account to take care of before we really dive into the wedding madness."

"Do I have to?" I whined, snuggling deeper into the couch. "I don't want to. I'll miss you too much."

"Yes, but I'm only going to be gone for three days. Then I'll be right back glued to your side," he promised, his voice soft and reassuring.

The next morning, we woke up at the crack of dawn, so Myles could make his 4 a.m. flight. I sleepily kissed him goodbye at the gate, watching him walk away with a tight knot in my chest.

The car door clicked shut behind him. Not wanting to make myself even more anxious, I pulled away from the airport. Myles's plane wouldn't take off for a while, but the tightness in my chest didn't loosen. This would be the longest time we would be apart since we have been together. Thanks to Sean, I won't be constantly staring at my phone waiting for him to text. We would instead be getting some key wedding details together. Hopefully, this would make dealing with Genevieve more bearable. But I still felt a little down. My apartment would be quiet without him, just me and my thoughts, which doesn't sound fun at all.

Sean had already been sending me texts all morning. Wedding planning, color schemes, and the usual reminders to not "let Myles's absence make me go crazy." I figured staying busy with her would help keep my mind off things. So, after a quick stop to grab snacks and wine, I headed over to her place.

"Alright, let's get this wedding stuff out of the way," Sean said, yanking open the door and pulling me inside like a tornado of energy.

We settled in at the kitchen table, a stack of wedding magazines and fabric swatches spread out before us. Sean popped open a can of soda. "You know, I was thinking about navy and blush pink."

I rolled my eyes. "That's so last year, everybody and their mamma has used that combination for some event. Not to mention isn't blush pink usually for baby showers."

"Fine, fine. How about lavender and silver?" she suggested with a playful grin.

I raised an eyebrow. "That's a hell no, no explanation needed. Not exactly the vibe we're going for. Plus those were your colors. I'm going to let you have that."

We went back and forth, each suggestion rejected with ridiculous reasons, but it was exactly what I needed. The laughter, the teasing, the feeling of normalcy. It made everything feel less heavy.

After a few hours of debating and laughing, we finally landed on sage green, gold, and ivory. "Perfect," Sean said, crossing out the other options on her notepad. "This is going to look so good with your skin tone."

I grinned. "You really can't go wrong with neutrals, and that was the one thing my baby asked me for. I think he has good taste."

She shot me a smirk. "Of course. He does, look who he's marrying!"

I felt the weight in my stomach lighten as the wedding details began to take shape. Still, there was that nagging feeling that wouldn't go away. I didn't want to admit it, but I was unnerved by how quiet the house would be tonight with Myles away. I checked my phone, nothing. I had not received a call, FaceTime, or text all day, which was strange because Myles should have landed hours ago.

As the evening wore on, I couldn't shake the feeling that something was off. So, I decided to do what any sane person would do. Snuggle up on the couch with my big ass bowl of popcorn and wine. Maybe, just maybe, that would put my mind at ease.

I sat there, remote in hand, flipping through channels. Nothing held my attention.

Nothing at all.

So I pulled out my phone, unlocking it without thinking to place a FaceTime call to Myles, just to hear his voice.

The call went straight to voicemail.

I tried again. Then again. And again.

Nothing. Not even a text. I told myself it was fine. Maybe his flight was delayed. Maybe he was busy with work, I don't know. I forced my mind to calm down, rationalizing away the anxiety creeping up my throat. "You'll hear from him in the morning," I muttered to myself. "Just go to bed, Lani. Everything's fine."

When the morning light crept through the curtains, I woke up with the same heavy feeling in my chest. I checked my phone, expecting a missed call or a message, but there was nothing. Not even a notification. I dialed his number again, only for it to go straight to voicemail. A chill ran down my spine.

My heart raced as I opened his location app. My fingers trembled as I swiped to refresh the page.

Sixteen hours ago, the app showed his location had last updated at my apartment. That was it.

I could feel the panic bubbling in my chest. Why hadn't he texted? Why hadn't he called? Where was he?

Suddenly, the TV blared to life as I flipped through the channels in a daze. The breaking news headline caught my attention. "Unidentified Male Body Discovered in Asheford River."

The words echoed in my ears. Male, late thirties, black. It felt like a punch to the gut.

Tears fell from my eyes before I could stop them. The room spun as the tears continued flowing, my worst fear clawing at me. Could it be? No. Myles was fine. He had to be.

I dialed Myles's number again, my hands shaking. FaceTime. Text message. Call after call, after call, all unanswered. The tightness in my chest turned into full-blown panic. He was supposed to be fine. He was just...gone for a few days. Right?

I needed to calm down. There was no reason to jump to conclusions. It's not him. It's not him.

But Darius, God, Darius was out there. And he was dangerous. I couldn't ignore the sinking feeling in my stomach. I tried to push it down, but it was like a weight pressing on my chest. I couldn't just sit here and do nothing.

I glanced at my phone, hoping for a text, a call, anything. There was nothing.

I needed to talk to Carlos. I couldn't raise Sean's blood pressure. She was pregnant, and I knew she was already stressed enough as it was.

With shaking hands, I called Carlos directly. The phone rang once, twice, before he picked up.

"Carlos, hey, have you heard from Myles?" I asked, trying to keep my voice steady, but my words felt thick. "He hasn't called to check in to tell me he landed anything."

He hesitated for a moment. "No, I haven't heard from him. Have you tried calling him?"

"Yes, of course I've called him a hundred times," I tried not to sound irritated. "I don't even want to think what could have happened. I don't know what to think. I... I saw that report on the news. About that body found in the river, my God, what if it was him?"

The silence on the other end of the line was suffocating. I felt my stomach twist into knots.

"Lani," Carlos said gently, "don't jump to conclusions. It's probably nothing. Myles is probably fine. It's just a coincidence."

I heard him trying to reassure me, but it didn't help. "Carlos, I have to go."

I disconnected the call. The bile in my throat rose, and I could feel the panic overtaking me. My legs buckled, and I barely made it to the bathroom before I vomited. The thought of something happening to Myles made me physically sick.

After a few moments, I wiped my mouth, sat on the cold bathroom floor, and leaned back against the wall, trying to steady my breathing.

I don't know how long I stayed there, but when I finally got up, I couldn't focus on anything. I couldn't eat. I couldn't drink. I couldn't think. It was all I could do to keep my phone charged, and close by, hoping, praying for some sign from Myles.

At least I was ahead of schedule with my bakery orders. And thank God, I had that rainy day footage saved on my phone. It wasn't much, but it gave me something to post on social media. Something to keep my presence up, but allowed me not to have to think. Even if it felt meaningless, it was something.

Hours passed in a blur. I dozed off at some point, but the moment I heard the pounding on my front door, I jumped out of bed, my heart racing. I stumbled to the door, barely able to make sense of my thoughts.

I threw it open, and there was Sean, looking a little panicked herself. "Lani! I've been knocking for ten minutes!" she exclaimed, rushing in before I even had a chance to speak. "You scared me to death."

I didn't even know what to say. I just let her pull me into a tight hug. Her arms wrapped around me, and for a moment, I felt safe again.

"Hold on," she said, pulling away, her face serious. "I've got to call Carlos. He's been worried sick too. When I didn't hear from you, I panicked, and called him over." She pulled out her phone, quickly dialing him.

I stood there, trying to get myself together, feeling like I was falling apart all over again. Sean spoke in a low voice, assuring Carlos that everything was okay, but I barely heard her.

"Did you hear anything else? Is there an update?" I asked, my voice barely above a whisper.

"No," she said, looking up from her phone. "No updates to the news report, nothing online, and no calls from Myles. I guess...that's good, right? I mean, if he was in trouble, we'd know by now. Right?"

I nodded slowly, trying to force myself to believe that. Sean's face softened as she approached me. "Myles is fine, Lani. There's probably a perfectly reasonable explanation for why he hasn't called. I bet it doesn't have anything to do with Darius."

"But what if it does?" I breathed, clutching my phone tightly in my hands. "What if something happened to him? What if..."

"Stop," Sean cut in, her voice firm, but kind. "You can't keep spiraling like this. Myles is fine. He's probably just...caught up with something. Maybe a delay, or he's busy with work. This is not about Darius."

I swallowed hard, the weight on my chest slowly easing, but just a little."Okay," I said quietly. "Okay, I just... I don't know what to think anymore."

Sean nodded, giving me one last reassuring squeeze. "He's fine, Lani. He's going to call you. And when he does, you'll feel a lot better, I promise."

I nodded, though the feeling of dread had settled in my gut wouldn't go away. It was hard to shake the fear. But Sean was right. There had to be an explanation. There had to be.

I had the whole day to get myself together before Myles's flight came in tomorrow evening. He was coming home, and I should've been excited, but all I could feel was anxiety creeping up my spine.

I stood in the middle of my living room and took in the chaos. The place looked like a depression room. Clothes were scattered everywhere from my failed attempt at laundry. Dishes piled up from half-hearted efforts to make myself eat. Everything was just…starts. Starts I never finished because worry consumed me.

It was bad. Worse than I'd ever let it get. For two days I hadn't even bothered to pick up after myself. Maybe it was because I couldn't sleep. Couldn't stop crying long enough to get anything done. Or maybe it was because every time I closed my eyes, I saw that damn body on the news.

But I wasn't going to let myself fall apart, not when Myles was on his way back. I had to have faith. I started picking up the clothes, shoving things into baskets. I wiped down countertops and vacuumed the carpet. Anything to keep myself busy, anything to stop the endless cycle of worry.

I bent down to grab a stray sock under the couch, and I hit my hand on something small and hard. I pulled it out; it was Myles's phone. Dead. My heart lurched in my chest, and my hand shook as I picked it up. The screen was black.

The knot in my stomach twisted tighter. I stared at the phone, feeling a cold sweat break out on the back of my neck.

This is why he didn't call or answer any of my calls. Why didn't he call anyone from the hotel phone? What if he'd had an emergency? He had no way to call for help.

This made everything feel much worse. I couldn't sit with this feeling any longer. I grabbed the phone and dialed Detective Imere's number. It rang twice before he answered.

"Detective Imere," his gravelly voice came through.

"Detective," I said quickly, trying to sound calm, but I was trembling. "It's Lani. I... I met you through the Darius McRay case. My fiancé has possibly gone missing, and I am terrified. Do you have any information on the body they pulled out of the river?"

There was a long pause on the other end. "Lani, unfortunately, that is not my case. I do not have any details I can share. How long has Mr. Parker been missing?"

"I dropped him off at the airport yesterday morning, and I have not heard from him since."

"I will admit, that is some what alarming, if you would like to file a missing persons report, you are free to come down to the station and do so. If your fiancé does in fact end up being missing, we will take it from there, but I would advise you not to worry. In these situations, no news really is good news."

"I understand, detective, but Myles left his phone in my apartment and has not attempted to contact me through any other means. He would not do that to me, especially with Darius out there being free."

Another long pause. "Lani, I understand you're worried, but I can't give you any details. You're going to have to wait until the authorities update the public. You just have to hang in there."

"Okay," I whispered, feeling like everyone was invalidating my feelings. "Thank you."

I hung up the phone slowly, not knowing whether to cry or scream. Myles was supposed to land tomorrow night. I had no choice but to wait until then. It wasn't like I had any other options. I couldn't sleep. I couldn't even fake it. The bags under my eyes were obvious, and every step felt like it took twice as long because I was so tired and dehydrated.

The next morning, I barely got out of bed. I sat there for a while, trying to figure out what to do. The house was still in disarray, but it looked better. I didn't have the energy to clean anymore. I could feel the weight of the world pressing down on me.

"Lani," I heard Sean's voice at the door, soft and gentle, "It's me. I'm coming in."

She stepped in, holding a bag of bagels and coffee. "We're going to get through this, okay?" she said, her voice filled with the quiet strength that always made me feel better, even when I didn't believe it myself.

I nodded, but it didn't make me feel any better. I had no appetite. My stomach was a pit of knots, and the thought of food made me want to throw up.

"Come on, eat something," Sean insisted, sitting beside me.

She handed me a cup of coffee and a bagel, nudging it toward me. "You need your strength. You can't do this on an empty stomach."

I forced myself to take a bite, but it felt like sand in my mouth. The taste was somewhere between nothing and cardboard. Sean had done her best bringing me my favorite, everything bagel with onion chive cream cheese. I just didn't have the capacity to register it.

I couldn't focus on anything. Not really. I couldn't stop thinking about Myles, about the possibility of him being out there, somewhere, in danger. About him being pulled from the river. The ending to our fragile new beginning. Even the possibility was earth-shattering for me.

When the time came to pick Myles up, I felt like I couldn't breathe. Carlos picked Sean and me up in his truck to take us to the airport. I was grateful for their presence, even if I wasn't ready to admit just how much I needed them. They couldn't know how much I was shaking on the inside.

We drove to the airport, the minutes stretching on forever. When we arrived, Myles's flight was delayed. Of course it was. The universe was definitely playing some kind of cruel joke on me.

Two hours passed, and I couldn't sit still. I paced around the terminal, checking my phone for any word. I was on edge, my thoughts racing. What if something had happened? What if he never made it?

And then, finally, I saw him. Myles walked through the gate, looking confused when he saw Sean and Carlos standing there with me. Then he took note of the look of anguish on my face. His face fell.

I felt my legs give out beneath me, and before I knew it, I was on the floor, tears streaming down my face.

Myles rushed over to me, kneeling beside me, panic flooding his eyes. "Lani, what's wrong? What happened? Are you okay?"

"I...I thought something...happened to you," I gasped, barely able to get the words out. "I...thought something...I thought you were..."

Myles's face went rigid as he made out exactly what I was trying to say. The moment it registered, he gently helped me to my feet. "No, no, I'm fine. I'm right here. Lani, what happened? What's going on? Why would you think that?"

Sean and Carlos took over, helping me steady myself, while Myles stayed close, his hand never leaving my arm. "Baby, I'm so sorry," he said, his voice full of regret. "I didn't mean to scare you. I forgot my phone at your apartment, I assume. I was in such a rush to get to the airport that I didn't even think about it. I didn't know any of your numbers by heart. It was a mess. By the time I realized I didn't have my phone, I tried to call the office, but everyone had left for the weekend. I didn't mean to make you worry, baby."

I shook my head, overwhelmed by everything. "I didn't know. I...I couldn't get a hold of you. The news, Myles. That body in the river, I thought,"

Myles kissed me gently on the forehead, his arms wrapped tight around me, like his embrace itself was a vow, a silent apology stronger than words.

"I'm sorry," he murmured. "I never meant for you to go through that. I should've thought it through, tried harder. I'll never forget my phone again, I promise. Better yet, I'll stop relying on it. Once I know you're okay, my next mission is learning everyone's number by heart."

I felt ridiculous. I was completely lost while Myles was gone. How could a detail that seemed so insignificant on the surface cause so much anxiety and fear? Something as trivial as not knowing a telephone number, something no one nowadays ever thinks about. Well, at least something I hadn't thought about. I closed my eyes, calming myself and letting his words sink in.

"I was so scared," I whispered.

"I know," he said softly. "But I'm here now. I'm safe. And I'll always make sure you know that."

The tension in my chest finally began to ease. Myles was home. Safe. And that was all that mattered.

Chapter 42

Once we got back to my apartment, I plopped down on the couch, mentally exhausted, but trying to force myself to relax. Myles sat next to me, flipping through channels, the soft hum of the TV filling the space around us. We didn't speak, just mindlessly watching, until a red banner scrolled across the screen.

BREAKING NEWS: BODY DISCOVERED IN RIVER.

I paused mid-sip, my wine glass frozen at my lips. Now that I knew for a fact the body found was not Myles, I should be fine, right? Wrong. I do not know why, but I had this gnawing, uneasy feeling about this whole situation.

The broadcaster's voice was steady, but grim as he continued. "...the body, recovered earlier this week, has yet to be identified. Authorities say foul play is suspected. More details to come."

I shivered, and for a moment, I couldn't shake the eerie chill crawling under my skin. Violent crimes weren't common around here. Murder? Even rarer. Stonebrook wasn't Mayberry, but it wasn't exactly a metropolis either. We had crime, but murder and dumping bodies were not an everyday occurrence.

I tried to push it aside, but the thought lingered, haunting me in the background. Both of us tired, him from work and traveling, me from stress, we both dozed off on the couch wrapped around each other like vines. I was grateful for the steady rhythm of Myles's breathing. He was strong, solid, and dependable. A perfect comfort.

At some point in the night, I felt him stir, and I opened my eyes just enough to see him smiling down at me. Not enough for him to know I wasn't asleep.

"This woman could sleep through an apocalypse," he whispered, his voice soft and amused. He scooped me into his arms, gently carrying me to bed.

I snuggled against him. It was moments like these that confirmed Myles's place in my life. The tenderness and thoughtfulness that he put into everything involving me. Even when it seemed no one was watching. I appreciated him in this moment especially, but also all the others since he came into my life.

Saturday morning, waking up with Myles beside me brought a sense of calm I hadn't felt all week. I was still a little wrecked from everything that had happened, but I managed to pull myself out of bed and head to the kitchen. Every step felt like moving through molasses, but I was determined to cook for my man. I wanted him to wake up to the sweet smell of breakfast.

I stood over the tray, inspecting my work like it was a work of art. Golden French toast dusted with powdered sugar, scrambled eggs, crispy bacon, and a steaming cup of Myles's favorite dark roast, breakfast fit for a king. I couldn't remember the last time I'd cooked like this, but I pushed the fatigue aside. This was for my fiancé!

I slipped back into the bedroom, holding the tray in front of me like I knew I just put my foot in this meal.

"This is for taking such good care of me. Even though you did leave me, didn't communicate with me for six days, and subsequently sent me spiraling into sadness, worry, and depression," I said softly, leaning down to kiss him, fighting hard to hold in my laughter. "Oh, and for loving me so thoroughly... when you remember."

"Now you know damn well... bring your butt over here." He rubbed his eyes, then glanced between me and the tray, his expression dazed. "Well, damn," he said in that husky morning voice I loved. "I don't know what to eat first."

I burst out laughing, swatting at him. "You sooo nastyyyy!"

He wiggled his brows at me before I retreated to the kitchen, his laughter following me like a warm blanket.

The rest of the day passed in a blur of wedding planning, venue tours with Genevieve, who was armed with her iPad, three backup chargers, as well as any and every checklist you could possibly think of. We visited three places, each more beautiful than the last, and each more impractical. Too many doors. Too many windows. Too many places for something or someone to go wrong.

It wasn't until we stepped into Paradise Gardens that I felt a deep exhale inside me, like a weight lifting from my chest.

The marble floors shimmered beneath the sun-dappled glass ceiling. A vine-covered dome let in golden light, casting a serene glow across everything. The fountain in the center whispered peace, its rhythm lulling me into a calm I hadn't realized I needed.

"This is it," I whispered, almost to myself.

Myles reached for my hand, giving it a gentle squeeze. "You sure?"

I nodded, my heart full. "I can see us here. I can feel it."

Genevieve clapped once, a grin spreading across her face. "Excellent! I'll get the contracts rolling."

By the time we made it back to Myles's place, I was exhausted, but oddly content. We shed our casual wear for pajamas, melting into the couch with our usual wine and snacks within reach. Just as I settled against his chest, the screen flashed again.

BREAKING NEWS: BODY FROM RIVER IDENTIFIED AS MICHAEL ROSS, 36, OF STONEBROOK.

The remote slipped from my hand and hit the floor with a soft thud. My heart skipped a beat. My breath caught in my throat.

"Michael?" I whispered, barely believing the words leaving my mouth.

Myles sat up straighter, his face serious now. "Michael Ross?"

I swallowed, my throat tight, and then the words came tumbling out, all at once. "Michael...my ex. The one who...who wrecked me. Who made me rebuild my life from scratch. Who stole years of my peace. That Michael."

Myles reached for my hands, gently holding them, his touch grounding me in the chaos of my mind.

"Baby," he said softly, his voice steady and calm. "I'm sorry, I know it is a shock that someone you knew was murdered, but this has nothing to do with you. It is unfortunate, but judging by your experiences you shared with me, he was not a good person."

I sat frozen, staring at the screen, the weight of it all crashing over me in waves. "I don't feel like it is my fault, and in the beginning I know I wished harm on him. He was absolutely terrible to me, but he didn't deserve to be murdered. I thought he needed to pay for how he treated me, but I didn't want this," I whispered. "Not like this."

Myles pulled me close, his arms wrapping around me in a protective embrace. "You didn't ask for it. But it happened. It's over just the same. Whatever shadow he had over your life, it is gone. Let it be gone."

I leaned against him, trying to soak in his warmth and comfort, but even as he whispered those words, a small voice in the back of my mind whispered something darker.

Things like this don't just happen.

Chapter 43

I sat at the kitchen table, a half-empty cup of tea cooling beside me, untouched. My eyes were unfocused, staring at everything and nothing all at once. The news of Michael's death had sunk into my bones like a chill I couldn't shake.

I hadn't loved him in a long time, not even close, but murdered? That didn't sit right with my spirit.

I spent hours rehashing our relationship. Not because I was grieving, but because I needed to understand. Michael had been selfish, arrogant, careless with my heart, sure. And he did get violent that one time. But still, dangerous? Deserving of that kind of ending?

It just didn't add up.

My thoughts kept circling back to the people he knew, the kind of life he led. Yeah, he had enemies. Who didn't? But I couldn't think of a single person who'd go so far as to kill him and dump him in a river.

I leaned back, arms crossed tightly across my chest. That's when a sharp knock split the silence, making me jump.

Heart racing, I checked the security cameras first, one of Myles's rules. His insistence was finally paying off.

Detective Imere stood on my doorstep, hands shoved deep in his coat pockets, his expression unreadable.

My brows drew together. If this were just an update, he could've called.

I cracked open the door. "Detective Imere. Are there any updates in the case?"

He nodded once, but his mouth was a grim line. "Sort of. May I come in?"

I stepped aside wordlessly.

Once we were settled in the living room, he wasted no time.

"You may have already heard that Michael Ross's body was discovered in the river."

I nodded, bracing myself. "I have."

He watched me carefully before going on. "We know you two were previously in a relationship."

I blinked, confused. "That's true, but… we've been done for a long time."

"I understand. That's not the issue. We have reason to believe Michael Ross's murder was committed by Darius McRay."

The room tilted.

"What?" The word escaped as a whisper. "No. No, how… why would you think that?"

"Mr. Ross was abducted. We have footage of Darius holding him at gunpoint before leading him to a white work van with no tags. Surveillance cuts out from there, but the timing aligns with Michael's death."

I stared at him, numb. Like the floor had cracked open beneath me. "He killed him?"

"We believe so. What's more concerning is how sloppy and violent it was. No effort to cover his tracks. That kind of recklessness usually signals a psychological break. A spiral. When someone starts acting without fear of consequence, it usually means one thing."

My mouth went dry. "A spree,"

I whispered. I had watched plenty of Criminal Minds to be able to grasp the concept of what was going on.

He nodded. "Exactly. And we believe you're the endgame."

I sank into the cushions. My ears rang. "But why now?"

Imere's expression softened, just barely. "We believe the trigger was your engagement. Congratulations, by the way. But to someone like Darius, that kind of news doesn't feel like closure. It feels like betrayal. We think this murder was a message. A twisted symbol of what he believes is love."

I could barely get air into my lungs. "But Michael, and I... we weren't close. Our breakup was messy, yes. But this? I didn't want this. Not like this."

"I know," Imere said gently. "But this isn't about real justice. It's Darius's warped version. His obsession has pushed him into dangerous territory, and he's showing he'll do anything to get your attention."

He handed me a card from his coat pocket. "We're increasing patrols around your area. If you have a security system, alert the company. And Ms. Shields, if you see him, or even think you do, call immediately. Do not hesitate."

I nodded numbly. As soon as the door closed behind him, I grabbed my phone to call Myles.

It was like he teleported.

The second he stepped through the door, he didn't wait. "Either you move in with me, or I move in with you. Your choice. But we're not spending another night apart. I do not care about your no living together rule. You are already going to be my wife at this point. There is no way you are spending another night out of my reach. If it comes to either one of us needing space, we just better go in the guest room, because this is happening."

I opened my mouth to argue, but nothing came out except a breath. "Okay."

"Okay? You're not going to fight me on this at all?" Myles looked at me curiously.

"No, as independent as I am, I'm scared, Myles."

I didn't fight him on this at all because deep down, I knew he needed to protect me, and if I'm being perfectly honest, I was scared as hell. I did not ever want to feel the way I did those three days when Myles was gone, and I could not reach him.

We planned everything over wine and snacks. Myles would handle the movers. I'd pack my essentials. His place had more space, more security, more of everything I needed to feel even remotely safe.

That night, we curled up in his bed, but sleep didn't come easily.

He sat up, reviewing contracts on his tablet, glasses perched low on his nose, chest bare under the amber glow of the bedside lamp. I watched him over the rim of a book I hadn't turned a single page in for twenty minutes.

I smiled.

"At least one good thing came out of all this," I murmured.

He looked over at me. "What's that?"

"I threw out my 'no living together until marriage' rule."

His smile was slow, wicked, and so familiar it made my heart ache.

He leaned over to kiss me, his lips warm and firm, grounding me in the moment.

Between kisses, he whispered, "Oh, for sure, that is definitely a plus."

I melted into his embrace, into the warmth, comfort, and love of this man. My man.

Chapter 44

The morning of the wedding bloomed with nerves and excitement. My heart was beating something fierce, nervously pounding as I sipped my mimosa in the bridal suite, wrapped in a silky white robe with "Bride" embroidered across the back. My girls fluttered around me, Sean, Joy, Kamryn, and Ava, laughing, sipping, and soaking up the glamour of the day. Genevieve had booked us with several of the hottest stylists in the city, so we had a team that buzzed through the room like bees, curling, pinning, brushing, blending.

"Girl, you better breathe," Joy teased, eyeing me as I tugged nervously at the ends of my freshly pressed curls. "You're getting married, this is supposed to be a beautiful, peaceful time for you. You have all these people in this room catering to your every need. Just relax, and let us handle everything."

I smirked, but the flutter in my stomach refused to settle. "I know, I know. I just... I want everything to go perfectly."

"It will," Sean said with a wink. "Even if it doesn't, you'll still be Mrs. Myles Parker by sundown. That's the only detail that really matters."

My phone buzzed on the table, and I dove for it.

A FaceTime: Myles.

I answered, and my heart smiled, the nerves I had before instantly calmed.

There he was, still sleepy, shirtless, hair all matted on one side, but still sexy in that effortless way he didn't even try to be.

"Morning, my almost-wife," he said, voice thick and low.

I grinned. "Morning, my barely-awake husband-to-be. You don't even look like someone who's getting married today."

He rubbed his eyes. "Your mattress is too damn soft. I swear I slept on a marshmallow smushed to four sticks. I'm too young for my back to be hurting like this. How have I never noticed before?"

I held up my mimosa. "Probably because you were blaming your soreness on…other things."

He gave me that crooked grin. "Now who's being nasty?"

His voice dipped. "You nervous?"

I hesitated, then nodded. "Yeah. But in the good way. You?"

"Terrified. But only because I want this to be everything you dreamed of."

My chest tightened. "It already is. Just… get here safe, okay?"

"You got it. I'm going to stop by the barber shop to get lined up, and I'll be there by four."

We hung up, both of us lingering for a second too long before hitting End.

By 4:00 p.m., the venue was a dream. Ivory florals cascaded from gold pillars. Candlelight flickered in tall glass vases. A string quartet played something soft and beautiful. The sun was beginning to dip low in the sky, casting everything in a golden haze.

There was no change in music to signal the groom or groomsmen had taken their places. No one came to tell me it was time to make my entrance. The only reason for that would be if Myles hadn't arrived. I slipped out of my suite quietly.

I didn't have to go far to see Carlos was pacing outside the groom's suite, muttering with his phone to his ear.

"Voicemail again? Shit!" he said, just before he called who I assumed was Sean.

I kept out of his line of sight because I knew he'd try to downplay Myles's absence. I needed to hear the truth for myself.

Carlos's voice was tight. "We can't find Myles. He said he was on his way at three. That was the last time I heard from him."

I went still. I knew he was not there, but hearing the actual words made the realization hit ten times worse. I wouldn't panic like I did when he went out of town. I slipped back into the bridal suite and plastered a fake smile on my face. I didn't want to worry anyone just yet, but I knew my girls knew something was up. When I entered, the laughter I had heard just moments before had started to fade. I checked my phone again. Still no message. Still no call.

At 5:45, the smile I'd been forcing started to crack.

By 6:05, I made my way into the vestibule, where I'd wait before walking down the aisle. As if by my being there, I could will Myles to appear. My palms were sweating.

Sean returned, smoothing her hands down the front of her emerald matron-of-honor gown like everything was fine.

"Okay," she said, her voice just a bit too high. "You ready to get married?"

I tried to smile. "Is he... here yet?"

She hesitated. Just a second too long.

My heart dropped. "Sean?"

Carlos slipped into the room, his face pale.

Sean exhaled slowly. "We haven't heard from him since three. But we're still trying. Carlos is calling everyone. Maybe his phone died again. You know how he is with that thing. We didn't want to worry you."

"I knew it. I tried to tell myself that I was overreacting and to let it all play out." My voice rose as I snatched my phone from the table. My fingers trembled as I called him myself.

Voicemail. Again.

A lump swelled in my throat. "He wouldn't do this to me. He wouldn't just disappear."

The music outside had started. If we were dealing with regular circumstances, that would be my cue. These circumstances, however, were not normal.

I didn't move.

"I'm not going out there," I snapped, eyes darting between them. "Not until I figure out what the hell is going on."

Sean stepped forward, placing her hands on my shoulders, and squeezed gently. "Lani, look at me. We're going to figure this out."

Sean and Carlos turned to go find Genevieve to alert the guests of the delay and to reassure them that everything was fine.

I sat there alone, lost in my thoughts.

I looked up just as the glass doors behind me opened.

Warm light poured into the room like melted gold.

A figure stood in the glow.

For a split second, my heart soared. "Myles?"

But as the door swung closed and the light shifted…

My stomach twisted.

He was wearing Myles's tux. He was a good two inches taller than Myles and had a thinner frame, so the fitting was noticeably off.

It was soaked in blood.

His hands, his shirt, his face, smeared in red. His eyes were wide and wild.

I screamed.

"Hello, beautiful," Darius said, his voice slow and dreamy "You didn't think I'd miss our big day, did you?"

All I could think about was Lani waiting for me at the altar, probably chewing on her lip and trying not to cry. That thought evaporated the second I saw that bastard.

Darius.

He was standing in the hallway like he owned it, as if he was waiting for me. Face slack, but eyes full, too full, like something unhinged was rattling behind his evil ass brain, consuming his thoughts. Before I could react, he shoved me back into the apartment, hard.

I stumbled back, slamming into the entry wall of Lani's apartment.

"What the hell?" I started, but he didn't let me finish.

He charged.

We collided like two football players on Super Bowl Sunday. His fist came fast, grazed my jaw, but I spun and caught him in the ribs with my elbow. He grunted but kept coming, grabbing my shirt and slamming me into the coffee table, sending a stack of books and a vase crashing to the floor.

I swung again, this time connecting solidly with his cheek. His head snapped back. Blood bloomed at the corner of his mouth.

"You think you can steal her from me?" he snarled, trying to knee me in the stomach. I caught his leg and shoved him backward, sending him crashing into the end table.

Glass shattered. I didn't stop. I lunged.

We grappled again, fists flying, crashing into the TV stand. I slammed him into the wall, pinning him with my forearm across his throat.

"She was never yours!" I shouted, chest heaving. "You're fucking sick!"

For a moment, he sagged under me. Face bruised. Breathing ragged. He looked defeated.

I started to reach for my phone with my free hand. And that's when I felt it. A sharp, burning sting in my leg.

"Son of a bitch, " I shouted, twisting to look.

Darius had pulled a syringe from his pocket, just that fast, and had already buried it in my thigh. I could feel the chemical fire racing through my veins as he pressed the plunger with vicious precision.

"You talk too much," he muttered.

I staggered back, my leg going numb. My vision blurred. The room tilted like a ship mid-storm.

I tried to swing again, but my arms refused to obey. My legs gave out, and I collapsed sideways against the wall, gasping, clawing at the floor, my body refusing to answer.

"You ruined everything," Darius whispered, crouching beside me, his breath sour and hot in my ear. "But I'll fix it. I always fix things."

I don't know how long I was out.

When I came to, the world was red.

Blood pooled around me, thick, drying, and sticky on my arms, my shirt, even the wall where he must've dragged me. I could feel shallow cuts, as well as deeper stab wounds all over my body. My back was propped against the living room wall. Drywall crumbled around me and on my shoulders from a dent in the wall. No doubt caused by him putting my head through it. The throbbing in the back of my head confirmed this. My legs were sprawled in front of me like I'd been discarded. Every inch of me hurt. Ribs, maybe cracked? My shoulder was definitely dislocated. My stomach was slick, tight, and hot.

I don't know how, but I was alive.

I tried to move.

Agony lanced through my body like fire licking bone. I let out a sound I didn't recognize, a raw and animalistic sound that scraped the silence.

I was dying.

I knew it. I could feel it. My breath was slower, my body sluggishly responding to my brain's commands. Each breath came jagged and shallow, like my lungs were folding in on themselves, one rib at a time. My body was shutting down, but there was still one thing anchoring me to this world.

Lani.

I couldn't leave her. Not like this. Not with that psycho out there.

I forced my fingers to move. They barely twitched against the hardwood, slick with blood, my blood. Oh my God, how did I let this happen? I'd dragged myself halfway to the front door before collapsing again. There was a trail behind me, crimson and glistening.

I coughed, and the taste of iron filled my mouth.

Get up. And move damnit.

The last thing I remembered before everything went black was Darius's face. His deranged eyes staring at me like he had won. His smile was completely unhinged and out of place. He had definitely taken a break from reality, which was even more reason I had to keep moving. I sat there trying to keep my mind strong by recalling details, trying to piece this shit together. I'd just stepped out of Lani's apartment, tux in hand, ready to head to the venue. The bastard had been waiting. Like a fucking apex predator. I was so caught up and ready to marry the love of my life that I abandoned all sense of my personal safety.

He must've had cameras on the building that he excessively watched; otherwise, there is no way he would know I was here. This apartment hadn't been used in months, not since Michael's body turned up. It was merely a glorified storage unit at this point.

Now here I was. Cuts everywhere. Ribs on fire. My tuxedo? Gone. Darius had stripped me of everything, like he was erasing me from the narrative.

I reached out, barely managing to brace against the edge of the coffee table. My fingers slipped, but found purchase long enough for me to glance toward the microwave clock.

6:14 p.m.

I was supposed to be at the altar by four.

My chest seized.

Lani.

I closed my eyes, and saw her, smiling, nervous, beautiful. Probably checking her phone for the hundredth time. Probably wondering if I was caught in traffic. Or worse, thinking I had second thoughts.

No.

No, not again. I wouldn't let her hurt. Not like this. Not because of me. And definitely not because of him. Darius wasn't going to win.

Chapter 46

Everything inside me turned to fire.

My heart beat so hard, it hurt. My breath came fast, shallow. The fabric of my gown scratched at my skin like thorns. Yet I remained still.

"Where is he?" I asked, my voice tight, cracking. "Where is Myles?"

He tilted his head, as if the question was confusing. "You're still thinking about him? Today's supposed to be about us."

"No," I whispered. "No, not anymore. I am sick of all of this shit."

Something inside me snapped.

I wasn't a victim. Not anymore. I wasn't going to be haunted by this man, not on my wedding day, not on any day, not ever again.

I moved without thinking. A blur of ivory satin and fury. I threw the first punch, and it landed right across his jaw. He stumbled back, startled, hands coming up to protect his face. I threw all the frustration from the past year into my fist, and willed them to connect. He might have thought he loved me as a soft, delicate flower, but today he was getting the beast.

Another punch, and another, blows landing against him like hail stones on unsuspecting cars. "What did you do?" I screamed "What did you do?"

Tears streamed down my face as I hit him again, my voice hoarse. "Where is he? Where is Myles?"

Darius grabbed my arms, trying to restrain me. His grip was too tight, his breathing heavy. "Stop," he growled, "Lani, stop."

And then something shifted in him.

His face went cold, stony. He looked at me like I wasn't real. Like I was something broken that needed to be punished.

He pushed me back at arm's length only, so he could draw back and backhand me.

Hard.

My head snapped to the side, and the world tilted. I crashed to the floor, vision swimming, ears ringing.

I felt him before I saw him. He knelt down to where my face was, fingers snatching my hair, yanking my head back so hard I saw stars.

"I loved you," he hissed, his voice shaking. "I hunted Michael for you, I tortured him, FOR YOU. When I was done, I cast him aside like the trash he was, FOR YOU. I did it all FOR YOU. I hoped you would see my worth, my devotion to you. I gave you the revenge that Myles never could. All for you to say fuck me and still choose him? What has he given you? Nothing! Cry...cry long and hard because I gutted that bitch like a fish in the home that was supposed to be ours!"

He yanked again, and I cried out.

"You betrayed me, Lani," he whispered, face inches from mine, breath hot and putrid. "I tried everything. Flowers, letters, waiting outside your apartment, sending messages. Giving you the fucking impossible, and nothing worked. You wouldn't see me, just like her. You wouldn't love me, just like her. But that's fine, I will just have to teach you like I taught her."

He dragged me closer to his face, straining my neck muscles even further, my neck at an impossible, dangerous angle.

"If you won't come willingly, then I have to change methods."

He slammed my head into the marble floor.

White exploded behind my eyes. My body went limp.

And just before everything went black, I saw the outline of him fading, like smoke, slipping into the shadows.

I stirred.

Voices were muffled, my head a battlefield of pain and confusion.

Sean was over me, sobbing. Her hands trembled as she touched my face, trying not to hurt me more.

Carlos hovered behind her, phone pressed to his ear, pacing like a man on the edge.

I tried to speak, but the words came slow and broken.

"Darius," I whispered. "My apartment…"

I couldn't remember why that mattered, only that it did.

I was watching myself from the outside, like a scene in a movie, floating just above my own body. Sean's face blurred, her mascara streaking down her cheeks. Carlos's voice sharpened.

"She said her apartment. Her APARTMENT, can you check if anyone's been there? Myles Parker, yes, unit 708."

Silence. And then Carlos froze.

He turned to us, eyes wide.

"They found the door open. Myles is there. He's alive, but barely."

Sean choked out a sob of relief.

Carlos crouched next to me. "Lani, you need an ambulance. Please, let me call them to help you."

I shook my head. Everything hurt, but none of it mattered.

"Take me to him," I said. My voice was weak, but I meant every word. "Take me now. You can have them check me out later. I need to see him."

Carlos looked at Sean, then back at me. She nodded.

"Okay. We'll get you to the hospital."

I closed my eyes again, just for a second.

Not to sleep, but to pray. I had watched enough movies to know that you never go to sleep after a head injury. But I needed to pray, God had to hear this one if he never heard another one. I prayed, and prayed some more that Myles would still be breathing by the time we arrived at the hospital.

The hospital was a cold, sterile place, and it felt like everything around me was pressing in, suffocating me slowly. The fluorescent lights flickered above, and the ticking of the clock on the wall was the only sound that broke through the maddening silence in my head. I couldn't focus on anything else but Myles, knowing he was in surgery, and all I could do was wait.

I couldn't sit still. I tried to stand and pace, but the dizziness from the head wound I had suffered quickly brought me back to reality. I sat again, but the movement didn't help. It didn't ease the tightness in my chest or the spinning of the room. I sat and closed my eyes to try to gain some type of stability. Sean and Carlos were there, but they might as well have been miles away, their words falling flat against the overwhelming silence inside my mind.

I glanced at the clock again. It felt like it had been an hour since we arrived, and I hadn't heard a word. My eyes darted to Sean, who was scrolling through her phone, trying to keep herself busy. Carlos, sitting across from me, was quiet, his eyes occasionally meeting mine, but I couldn't seem to focus on anything. I could tell they wanted to say it, but both were afraid of upsetting me.

"Are you sure you're okay?" Sean asked, finally glancing up from her phone, her voice soft but concerned.

I shook my head, not trusting myself to speak. The weight of the worry I felt for Myles was crushing, and I didn't know how to keep it together.

"You look pale, Lani. That gash on your forehead is very angry, and you could have a concussion," Sean pressed, her tone gentle but insistent. "Let the doctors check you out, just to be safe. You at least need to see to the gash."

"I'm fine," I muttered, trying to push the fear and exhaustion away. "I just need to know about him. I need to know that he's going to be okay."

"We can let the nurses know that we will be in the ER, so if there is an update before we can make it back here, they know where to find you, but you have got to have that looked at," Sean said while motioning toward the wound on my head.

"I know you want to be available, I get that. But you're not going to be any help to him if you collapse from a concussion or pain yourself. Now come on, let's just go and get you checked out."

I didn't argue, because she was right, but the idea of being pulled away from the waiting area, from the only thing I could focus on right then, felt like a betrayal. Still, Sean was right, and I knew it. I nodded, feeling weak, and allowed her to lead me toward the ER.

The doctor did a quick assessment, asking me questions I barely heard. She was calm, methodical, and soon enough, as expected, she ordered a CT scan. Once finished, I sat in the cold, uncomfortable chair, waiting for the results, my fingers twisted in my lap. The machine hummed as the scan was done, and the cold sensation of the contrast fluid made my skin prickle. All I could think about was Myles. What was happening to him, if he was still fighting.

After what felt like an eternity, the doctor returned, and I held my breath as she spoke.

"You're in the clear," she said, relief washing over me, though it didn't quiet the storm of worry inside. "You have no major damage to your brain or skull. But I do want to give you something for pain and stitch up that nasty gash on your forehead."

I nodded, too relieved to respond properly, and let her do what she needed to do. The sting of the stitches was nothing compared to the storm raging in my chest. I barely felt it as she worked, her hands steady, her calm professionalism a stark contrast to my spiraling emotions.

After the stitches were complete, I made a beeline for the surgical waiting rooms. As soon as I got there, I gave into gravity and fell into the chair, more tired than I had ever been in my life. I didn't know if it was because of the extremely tough day I was having or the pain medication the doctor gave me. Either way, I listened to my body and had a seat. I tried to steady my breathing, to gather myself, but the room was spinning. The clock ticked away, each second stretching on forever, and still, there was no word on Myles. I couldn't shake the feeling that time was slipping away from me, and that every second he was in surgery was a second too long.

I hadn't been in the waiting area ten minutes before Detective Imere walked in, his face somber. He didn't sit, just stood there, his eyes scanning the room before locking onto me.

"Ms. Shields," he began, his tone heavy. "I need to get your statement."

I nodded slowly, though my throat felt tight. I took a deep breath, and the words started tumbling out, recounting everything from the moment Darius showed up at our wedding. I told him how he confessed to hunting and killing Michael, how he told me he had gutted Myles. That last revelation was hard to repeat. For a moment there, I thought the words would be stuck in my throat. I described how his words, his intentions, became darker, more dangerous. I explained how I feared for my life, how it felt like he was no longer trying to protect me, or shower me with his warped sense of love, but more so possess me, punish me for not choosing him.

When I finished recounting it all, Detective Imere just stood there, silent for a moment. His face was grim, his eyes calculating as if weighing the weight of my words and carefully trying to choose his.

"I'm not trying to scare you when I say this, Ms. Shields," he said, his voice low and serious, "but I think this situation has become more grave for you. Mr. McRay has escalated. What started as him thinking he was your protector, or your lover, has turned into something far more dangerous. You are right in assuming he wants to possess you, to punish you. With the way he's been able to evade us, you need to be extra careful. You need to be vigilant, report anything suspicious immediately. Your life, or Mr. Parker's life, could depend on it."

I felt the air leave my lungs, the words pressing down on me like a heavy weight. Possess and punish. The words echoed in my head, and I couldn't seem to shake the chill that spread through me.

"I'll be in touch," Detective Imere added, his expression hardening as he turned to leave. "Just stay alert, Ms. Shields. This isn't over."

And then he was gone, leaving me in the quiet, oppressive silence.

The minutes dragged by. I barely noticed Sean and Carlos speaking to me, their voices muffled in the background. I couldn't focus on anything but the gnawing fear that Darius was still out there, waiting, watching, plotting his next move.

Hours passed before the doctor came in with an update on Myles. He was wearing surgical scrubs, his face tired, his voice quiet.

"We've managed to stop the major bleeding," he said, his eyes avoiding mine. "He has some organ damage, but we have stabilized him. Unfortunately, he has suffered damage to his brain, the extent of which we won't know until he wakes up. He has several broken bones that we have managed to set. As for his wounds, we were able to close them all, deep and shallow. The wounds to his stomach were particularly concerning and could lead to possible long-term damage... we just do not know yet. We are watching him carefully, trying to be proactive. He's in critical condition, and we have sedated him heavily to give his body time to heal."

I nodded, my body feeling heavy, drained. My mind was still caught on the words critical condition.

"When he wakes, he will be in immense pain. We will keep him under as long as we can to try to minimize this," the doctor continued. "He'll be in ICU for a while. I need you to manage your expectations. This is not a situation where he wakes up and is home the next day. He will need months of rehabilitation. That is if he makes it through the night."

I barely heard the last part, the rest of his words drowned out by the rush of fear tempered with some relief and grief. All these emotions flooded my chest. I couldn't hold it in any longer. I collapsed to the floor, the tears spilling over, my body wracked with sobs.

I cried for Myles, for the pain he was in, for the hell he was going to face when and if he woke up. But there was also a deep sense of gratitude. He was alive.

See you in Tethered by Lies...

I hope you have enjoyed Lani, and Myles's journey, so far, Please leave a review. I would greatly appreciate the feedback.

Subscribe to my newsletter at www.kristenchace.com for all updates.

Also my YouTube channel: **Kristen Chace** to hear readings of this selection, and more.

Acknowledgement

To everyone who I spoiled the plot of this book for, but still read it! Y'all know I can't hold water! I promise next time it won't be like this!

www.ingramcontent.com/pod-product-compliance
Lightning Source LLC
Chambersburg PA
CBHW021426110726
47901CB00008B/2322